The Murder
of Delicia

The Murder of Delicia

Marie Corelli

MINT EDITIONS

The Murder of Delicia was first published in 1896.

This edition published by Mint Editions 2021.

ISBN 9781513277790 | E-ISBN 9781513278209

Published by Mint Editions®

MINT
EDITIONS

minteditionbooks.com

Publishing Director: Jennifer Newens
Design & Production: Rachel Lopez Metzger
Project Manager: Micaela Clark
Typesetting: Westchester Publishing Services

Contents

I

A flood of warm spring sunshine poured its full radiance from the south through the large, square lattice-window of Delicia's study, flashing a golden smile of recognition on Delicia herself and on all the objects surrounding her. Gleaming into the yellow cups of a cluster of daffodils which stood up, proudly erect, out of a quaint, brown vase from Egypt, it flickered across a pearl-inlaid mandoline that hung against the wall, as though it were playing an unheard melody in delicate *tremolo* on the strings; then, setting a crown of light on Delicia's hair, it flung an arrowy beam at the head of Hadrian's 'Antinous,' whose curved marble lips, parted in an inscrutable, half-mocking smile, seemed about to utter a satire on the ways of women. Delicia had purchased this particular copy of the original bust in the British Museum because she imagined it was like her husband. No one else thought it in the least like him—but she did.

She had all sorts of fancies about this husband of hers—fancies both pretty and passionate—though she had none about herself. She was only a worker; one whom certain distinguished noodles on the Press were accustomed to sneer at from their unintellectual and impecunious standpoint as 'a lady novelist' not meriting the name of 'author,' and who, despite sneers and coarse jesting, was one of the most celebrated women of her time, as well as one of the wealthiest. The house she lived in, built from her own designs, furnished with every luxury and filled with valuable pictures, curios and art-treasures, was one of the material results of her brilliant brain-work; the perfectly-ordered *ménage*, the admirably-trained servants, the famous 'table' at which many of London's most fastidious *gourmets* had sat and gorged themselves to repletion, were all owing to her incessant and unwearying labour. She did everything; she paid everything, from the taxes down to the wages of the scullery-maid; she managed everything, from the advantageous disposal of her own manuscripts down to the smallest detail of taste and elegance connected with the daily serving of her husband's dinner. She was never idle, and in all her literary efforts had never yet failed to score a triumph above her compeers.

As a writer, she stood quite apart from the rank and file of modern fictionists. Something of the spirit of the Immortals was in her blood—the spirit that moved Shakespeare, Shelley and Byron to proclaim truths in the face of a world of lies—some sense of the responsibility and worth of Literature—and with these emotions existed also the passionate desire to rouse and exalt her readers to the perception of the things she herself knew and instinctively felt to be right and just for all time. The public responded to her voice and clamoured for her work, and, as a natural result of this, all ambitious and aspiring publishers were her very humble suppliants. Whatsoever munificent and glittering 'terms' are dreamed of by authors in their wildest conceptions of a literary El Dorado, were hers to command; and yet she was neither vain nor greedy. She was, strange to say, though an author and a 'celebrity,' still an unspoilt, womanly woman.

Just when the sunshine crowned her, as the sunshine had a way of doing at that particular hour of the morning, she was very busy finishing the last chapter of a book which had occupied all her energies during the past four months. She wrote rapidly, and the small, well-shaped, white hand that guided the pen held that dangerous intellectual weapon firmly, with a close and somewhat defiant grip, suggestive of the manner of a youthful warrior grasping a light spear and about to hurl it in the face of a foe. Her very attitude in writing indicated mental force and health; no 'literary stoop' disfigured her supple back and shoulders, no sign of 'fag' or 'brain-muddle' clouded the thoughtful yet animated expression of her features. Her eyes were bright, her cheeks delicately flushed. She had no idea of her own poetic and unique loveliness, which was utterly unlike all the various admitted types of beauty in woman. She scarcely knew that her eyes were of that divinely rare, dark violet colour which in certain lights looks almost black, that her skin was white as a snowdrop, or that her hair, in its long, glistening masses of brown-gold, was a wonder and an envy to countless numbers of her sex who presented themselves to the shrewdly-grinning gaze of the world with dyed 'fronts' and false 'back coils.' She truly never thought of these things. She had grown to understand, from current 'smart' newspaper talk, that all authoresses, without exception, were bound to be judged as elderly and plain, even hideous, in the matter of looks, according to the accepted conventional standard of 'press' ethics, and though she was perfectly aware that she was young, and not as repulsive in her personal appearance as she ought to be for the profession of letters, she took very little trouble to assert herself, and made no attempt whatever to 'show off her points,' as the slang parlance hath it, though those 'points' outnumbered in variety and charm the usual attractions of attractive women. Admirers of her genius were too dazzled by that genius to see anything but the glow of the spiritual fire burning about her like the Delphic flames around Apollo's priestess, and the dainty trifles of personality, which are ordinarily all a woman has to boast of, were in her case lost sight of. Compliments and flatteries, however, were distasteful to her, except when on rare occasions she received them from her husband. Then her sweet soul kindled within her into a warm glow of rapture and gratitude, and she wondered what she had done to deserve praise from so lordly and perfect a being.

There was something very touching as well as beautiful in the way Delicia bent her proud intellect and prouder spirit to the will of her chosen mate. For him, and for him only, she strove to add fresh glory to the lustre of her name; for him she studied the art of dressing perfectly, loving best to drape herself in soft white stuffs that clung in close, artistic folds round her light and lissom figure, and made her look like a Greuze or a Romney picture; for him she took pains to twist the rich treasure of her hair in cunning braids and love-locks manifold, arranging it in a soft cluster on her fair forehead after the fashion of the ancient Greeks, and scattering here and there one or two delicate rings about her finely-veined temples, as golden suggestions of kisses to be pressed thereon. For him she cased her little feet in fascinating *brodequins* of deftest Paris make; for him she moved like a sylph and smiled like an angel; for him she sang, when the evenings fell, old tender songs of love and home, in her rich, soft contralto; for him indeed she lived, breathed and—worked. She was the hiving bee—he the luxurious drone that ate the honey. And it never occurred to him to consider the position as at all unnatural.

Certainly Delicia loved her work—of that there could be no doubt. She enjoyed it with every fibre of her being. She relished the keen competition of the literary arena, where her rivals, burning with jealousy, endeavoured vainly to emulate her position; and she valued her fame as the means of bringing her into contact with all the leading men and women of her day. She was amused at the small spites and envies of the malicious and unsuccessful, and maintained her philosophical and classic composure under all the trumpery slights, ignorant censures and poor scandals put upon her by the less gifted of her own sex. Her career was one of triumph, and being sane and healthy, she enjoyed that triumph to the full. But more than triumph, more than fame or the rewards of fame, more indeed than all things in the world ever devised, measured or possessed, she loved her husband,—a strange passion for a woman in these wild days when matrimony is voted 'out of date' by certain theory-mongers, and a 'nobleman' can be found ready to give a money-bribe to any couple of notoriety-hunters who will consent to be married in church according to the holy ordinance, and who will afterwards fling a boorish insult in the face of Religion by protesting publicly against the ceremony. Delicia had been married three years, and those three years had passed by like three glittering visions of Paradise, glowing with light, colour, harmony and rapture. Only one grief had clouded the pageant of her perfect joy, and this was the death of her child, a tiny mortal of barely two months old, which had, as it were, dropped out of her arms like a withered blossom slain by sudden frost. Yet, to Delicia's dreamy and sensitive temperament, the sadness of this loss but deepened her adoration for him round whom her brilliant life twined like a luxurious vine full of blossom and fruit—the strong, splendid, bold, athletic, masterful creature who was hers—hers only! For she knew—her own heart told her this—that no other woman shared his tenderness, and that never, never had his faith to her been shaken by so much as one unruly thought!

And thus it was that Delicia often said of herself that she was the happiest woman in the world, and that her blessings were so many and so various that she was ashamed to pray. 'For how can I, how dare I ask God for anything else when I have so much?' she would inwardly reflect. 'Rather let me be constant in the giving of thanks for all the joys so lavishly bestowed upon me, which I so little deserve!' And she would work on with redoubled energy, striving after perfection in all she did, and full of a strange ardour combined with a yet stranger humility. She never looked upon her work as a trouble, and never envied those of her own sex whose absolute emptiness of useful occupation enabled them to fritter away their time in such 'delightful' amusements as bicycling, rinking, skirt-dancing and other methods of man-hunting at present in vogue among the fair feminine animals whose sole aim of existence is marriage, and after that—nullity. Her temperament was eminently practical as well as idealistic, and in the large amounts of money she annually earned she never lost a penny by rash speculation or foolish expenditure. Lavish in her hospitalities, she was never ostentatious, and though perfect in her dress, she was never guilty of the wild and wicked extravagance to which many women in her position and with her means would have yielded without taking a moment's thought. She carefully considered the needs of the poor, and helped them accordingly, in secret, and without the petty presumption of placarding her charities to the world through the medium of a 'bazaar' or hypocritical 'entertainment at the East End.' She felt the deep truth of the saying, 'Unto whom much is given, even from him shall much be required,' and gave her largesse with liberal tenderness and zeal. On one point alone did she outrun the measure of prudence in the scattering of her wealth, and this was in the consideration of her husband. For him nothing was too good, nothing too luxurious, and any wish he expressed, even by the merest chance, she immediately set herself, with pride and joy, to gratify. As a matter of fact, he had not really a penny to call his own, though his private banking account always showed a conveniently large surplus, thanks to Delicia's unfailing care. Wilfred de Tracy Gifford Carlyon, to give him all his names in full, was an officer in the Guards, the younger son of a nobleman who had, after a career of wild extravagance, died a bankrupt. He had no other profession than the military, and though a man of good blood and distinguished descent, he was absolutely devoid of all ambition, save a desire to have his surname pronounced correctly. 'Car*lee*-on,' he would say with polite emphasis, 'not Car-*ly*-on. Our name is an old, historical one, and like many of its class is spelt one way and pronounced another.'

Now, without ambition, the human organisation becomes rather like a heavy cart stuck fast in the mud-rut it has made for itself, and it frequently needs a strong horse to move it and set it jogging on again. In this case, Delicia was the horse; or, to put it more justly, the high-spirited mare, galloping swiftly along an open road to a destined end, and scarcely conscious of the cart she drew at such a rattling pace behind her. How indignant she would have been had she overheard any profane person using this irreverent cart simile in connection with her one supremely Beloved! Yet such was the true position of things as recognised by most people around her; and only he and she were blind to the disproportionate features of their union; she with the rare and beautiful blindness of perfect love, he with the common every-day blindness of male egotism.

That he had exceptional attractions of his own wherewith to captivate and subdue the fair sex was beyond all question. The qualities of 'race,' derived from a long ancestral line of warriors and statesmen, had blossomed out in him physically if not mentally. He had a fine, admirably-moulded figure, fit for a Theseus or a Hercules, a handsome face and a dulcet voice, rich with many gradations of persuasive and eloquent tone. Armed with these weapons of conquest, he met Delicia at the moment when her small foot had touched the topmost peak of Fame, and when all the sharp thorns and icicles of the strange crown wherewith Art rewards her chosen children were freshly set among her maiden hair. Society thought her a chilly vestal—shrank from her, indeed, somewhat in vague fear; for her divine, violet eyes had a straight way of looking through the cunningly-contrived mask of the social liar, and, like the 'Rontgen rays,' taking a full impression of the ugly devil behind it. Society refused to recognise her ethereal and half elfin type of beauty. It 'could see nothing in her.' She was to it 'a curious sort of woman, difficult to get on with,'—and behind her back it said of her the usual mysterious nothings, such as, 'Ah! one never knows what those kind of persons are!' or, 'Who *was* she?' and, 'Where does she get her strange ideas from?'—slobbering its five o'clock tea and munching its watercress sandwiches over these scrappy suggestions of scandal with a fine relish only known to the 'upper class' matron and the Whitechapel washerwoman. For however much apart these two feminine potentialities may be in caste, they are absolutely one in their love of low gossip and slander.

Nevertheless, the dashing Guards officer, who had been flung into an expensive regiment at the reckless whim of his late father, found several engaging qualities in Delicia, which appealed to him partly on account of their rarity, and partly because he, personally, had never been able to believe any woman capable of possessing them. Perhaps the first of the various unique characteristics he recognised in her, and marvelled at, was her total lack of vanity. He had never in all his life before met a pretty woman who attached so little importance to her own good looks; and he had certainly never come across a really 'famous' personage who wore the laurels of renown so unconsciously and unassumingly. He had once in his life had the honour of shaking hands with an exceedingly stout and florid poetess, who spoke in a deep, masculine voice, and asked him what he thought of her last book, which, by-the-bye, he had never heard of, and he had also lunched in the distinguished company of a 'sexual fictionist,' a very dirty and dyspeptic-looking man, who had talked of nothing else but the excellence and virtue of his own unsavoury productions all through the course of the meal. But Delicia!—Delicia, the envy of all the struggling, crowding climbers up Parnassus,—the living embodiment of an almost phenomenal triumph in art and letters—Delicia said nothing about herself at all. She assumed no 'airs of superiority;' she talked amusing trifles like other less brilliant and more frivolous people; she was even patient with the ubiquitous 'society idiot,' and drew him out with a tactful charm which enabled him to display all his most glaring points to perfection; but when anyone began to praise her gifts of authorship, or ventured to comment on the wide power and influence she had attained through her writings, she turned the conversation instantly, without *brusquerie* but with a gentle firmness that won for her the involuntary respect of even the flippant and profane.

This unpretentious conduct of hers, so exceptional in 'celebrities,' who, in these days of push-and-scramble have no scruples about giving themselves what is called in modern parlance 'any amount of side,' rather astonished the gallant 'Beauty Carlyon,' as he was sometimes nicknamed by his fellow officers; and, as it is necessary to analyse his feelings thoroughly, it must also be conceded that another of his sensations on being introduced to the woman whose opinions and writings were the talk of London, was one of unmitigated admiration mingled with envy at the thought of the fortune she had made and was still making. What!—so slight a creature, whose waist he could span with his two hands, whose slender neck could be wrung as easily as that of a singing-bird, and whose head seemed too small for its glistening weight of gold hair—she, to be the possessor of a name and fame reaching throughout every part of the British Empire, and far across the wide Atlantic, and the independent mistress of such wealth as made his impecunious mouth water! Ten thousand pounds for her last book!—paid down without a murmur, even before the work was finished!—surely 'these be excellent qualities,' he mused within himself, afterwards falling into a still more profound reverie when he heard on unimpeachable authority that the royalties alone on her already-published works brought her in an income of over five thousand a year. Her first book had been produced when she was but seventeen, though she had feigned, when asked, to be several years older, in order to ensure attention from publishers; and she had gone on steadily rising in the scale of success till now—when she was twenty-seven, and famous with a fame surpassing that of all her men contemporaries. No doubt much money had been put by during those ten triumphal years!

Taking all these matters into consideration, it was not to be wondered at that the penniless Guardsman thought often and deeply concerning the possibilities and advantages of Delicia as a wife, and that, during the time he formed one of the house-party among whose members she was the most honoured guest, he should seize every opportunity of making himself agreeable to her. He began to study her from a physical point of view, and very soon discovered in her a charm which was totally unlike the ordinary attractiveness of ordinary women. In strict fairness to him, it must be admitted that his realisation of Delicia's fine and delicate nature was due to distinctly sincere feeling on his part, and was not inspired by any ulterior thought of Mammon. He liked the way she moved; her suave, soft step and the graceful fold and flow of her garments pleased him; and once, when she raised her eyes suddenly to his in quick response to some question, he was startled and thrilled by the glamour and sweet witchery of those dark purple orbs, sparkling with such light as can only be kindled from a pure soul's fire. Gradually he, six feet of man, nobly proportioned, with a head which might be justly termed classic, even heroic, though it lacked certain bumps which phrenology deems desirable for human perfection—fell desperately in love, and here his condition must be very positively emphasised, lest the slightest doubt be entertained of it hereafter. To speak poetically, the fever of love consumed him with extraordinary violence night and day; and the strongest form of that passion known to men, namely, the covetous greed of possession, roused him to the employment of all his faculties in the task of subduing the Dian-like coldness and crystalline composure of Delicia's outward-seeming nature to that tenderness and warmth so eminently desirable in a woman who is, according to the dictum of old Genesis, meant to be a man's helpmate, though the antique record does not say she is to be so far helpful as to support him altogether. Among the various artful devices Carlyon brought to his somewhat difficult attack on the ivory castle of a pure, studious and contemplative maidenhood, were a Beautiful Sullenness,—a Dark Despair,—and a Passionate Outbreak—the latter he employed at rare intervals only. When the Beautiful Sullenness was upon him he had a very noble appearance; the delicate, proud curve of his upper lip was prominent,—his long, silky lashes, darkly drooping, gave a shadow of stern sweetness to his eyes; and Delicia, glancing at him timidly, would feel her heart beat fast, like the fluttering wing of a frightened bird, if he chanced to raise those eyes from their musing gloom and fix them half-ardently, half-reproachfully on her face. As for the Dark Despair, the sublimity of aspect he managed to attain in that particular mood could never be described in ordinary language; perhaps, in the world's choicest galleries of art, one might find such a wronged and suffering greatness in the countenance of one of the sculptured gods or heroes, but surely not elsewhere. However, it was the Passionate Outbreak,— the lightning-like fury and determination of mere manhood, springing forth despite the man himself, and making havoc of all his preconceived intentions, that won his cause for him at last. The moment came—the one moment which, truly speaking, comes but once to any human life; the pre-ordained, divine moment, brief as the sparkle of foam on a breaking wave,—the glimpse of Heaven that vanishes almost before we have looked upon it. It was a night never to be forgotten—by Delicia, at least; a night when Shakespeare's elves might have been abroad, playing mischief with the flowers and scattering wonder-working charms upon the air—a true 'Midsummer Night's Dream' which descended, full-visioned in silver luminance, straight from Paradise for Delicia's sake. She was, at that time, the guest of certain 'great' people; the kind of 'great' who say they 'must have a celebrity or two, you know!—they are such queer, dear things!' Delicia, as a 'queer, dear thing,' was one of the celebrities thus entertained, and Pablo de Sarasate, also as a 'queer, dear thing,' was another. A number of titled and 'highly-connected' personages, who had the merit of being 'queer' without being in the least 'dear,' made up the rest of the party. The place they were staying at was a lordly pile, anciently the 'summer pleasaunce' and favourite resort of a great Norman baron in the days of Richard the Lion-hearted, and the grounds extending round and about it were of that deep-shadowed, smooth-lawned and beautifully sylvan character which only the gardens of old, historic English homes possess. Up and down, between a double hedge of roses, and under the radiance of a golden harvest moon, Delicia moved slowly with Carlyon at her side; and from the open drawing-room windows of the house floated the pure, penetrating voice of Sarasate's violin. Something mystic in the air; something subtle in the scent of the roses; a stray flash of light on the falling drops of the fountain close by, which perpetually built and unbuilt again its glittering cupola of spray, or some other little nothing of the hour, brought both man and woman to a sudden pause,—a conscious pause, in which they each fancied they could hear their own hearts beating loudly above the music of the distant violin. And the man,—the elected son of Mars, who had never yet lifted his manhood to the height of battle, there to confront horror upon horror, shock upon shock,—now sprang up full-armed in the lists of love, and, strong with a strength he had hardly been aware of as existing in himself before, he swiftly and boldly grasped his prize.

'Delicia!' he whispered—'Delicia, I love you!'

There was no audible answer. Sarasate's violin discoursed suitable love-passages, and the moon smiled as if she would have spoken, but Delicia was silent. She had no need of speech—her eyes were sufficiently eloquent. She felt herself drawn with a passionate force into her lover's strong arms, and clasped firmly, even jealously, to his broad breast; and like a dove, which after long journeyings finds its home at last, she thought she had found hers, and folding her spirit-wings, she nestled in and was content.

Clinging to this great and generous protector who thus assumed the guardianship of her life, she marvelled innocently at her own good fortune, and asked herself what she had done to deserve such ineffable happiness. And he? He too, at this particular juncture, may be given credit for nobler emotions than those which ordinarily swayed him. He was really very much in love; and Love, for the time being, governed his nature and made him a less selfish man than usual. When he held Delicia in his arms, and kissed her dewy lips and fragrant hair for the first time, he was filled with a strange ecstasy, such as might have moved the soul of Adam when, on rising from deep sleep, he found embodied Beauty by his side as 'help-meet' through his life for ever. He was conscious that in Delicia he had won not only a sweet woman, but a rare intelligence; a spirit far above the average,—a character tempered and trained to finest issues,—and from day to day he studied the grace of her form, the fairness of her skin, the lustre of her eyes, with an ever-deepening intensity of delight which imparted a burning, masterful ardour to the manner of his wooing, and brought her whole nature into a half-timid, half-joyous subjection—the kind of subjection which might impel a great queen to take off her crown and lay it at the feet of some splendid warrior, in order that he might share her throne and kingdom. And in this case the splendid warrior was only too ready to accept the offered sovereignty. Certainly he loved Delicia; loved her with very real and almost fierce passion,—the passion that leaps up like a tall, bright flame, and dies down to a dull ember; but he could hardly be altogether insensible to the advantages he personally gained by loving her. He could not but exult at the thought that he, with nothing but his handsome appearance and good birth to recommend him, had won this woman whose very name was a lode-star of intellectual attraction over half the habitable globe, and, in the very midst of the ardent caresses he lavished upon her, he was unable to entirely forget the fortune she had made, and which she was adding to every day. Then she was charming in herself, too—lovely, though not at all so according to the accepted 'music-hall' standard of height and fleshy prominence; she was more like the poet's dream of 'Kilmeny in Fairyland' than the 'beauty' of eighteenpenny-photograph fame; but she was, as Carlyon himself said, 'as natural as a rose—no paint, no dye, no purchased hair cut from the heads of female convicts, no sickly perfumes, no padding, nothing in the least artificial about her.' And hearing this, his particular 'chum' in the Guards Club said,—

'Lucky dog! You don't deserve such a "draw" in the matrimonial lottery!'

And Carlyon, smiling a superior smile, looked in a conveniently near mirror, and replied,—

'Perhaps not! But—'

A flash of the fine eyes, and a touch of the Beautiful Sullenness manner finished the sentence. It was evident that the gallant officer was not at all in doubt as to his own value, however much other folks might be disposed to consider the pecuniary and other advantages of his marriage as altogether exceeding his merits.

Yet, on the whole, most people, with that idiotic inconsistency which characterises the general social swarm, actually pitied him when they heard what was going to happen. They made round eyes of astonishment, shook their heads and said, 'Poor Carlyon!' Why they made round eyes or shook their heads, they could not themselves have explained, but they did so. 'Poor,' Carlyon certainly was; and his tailor's bill was an appalling one. But 'they,'—the five-o'clock-tea gossips, knew nothing about the tailor's bill—that was a private affair,—one of those indecent commonplaces of life which are more or less offensive to persons of high distinction, who always find something curiously degrading in paying their tradesmen. 'They' saw Carlyon as he appeared to them—superb of stature, proud of bearing, and Greekly 'god-like' of feature—and that he was always irreproachably dressed was sufficient for them, though not for the unpaid tailor who fitted him so admirably. Looking at him in all his glory, 'they' shuddered at the thought that he—this splendid specimen of manhood—was actually going to marry a—what?

'A novelist, my dear! just think of it!' feebly screamed Mrs. Tooksey over her Queen Anne silver teapot. 'Poor Wilfred Carlyon! Such a picturesque figure of a man! How awful for him!'

And Mrs. Snooksey, grabbing viciously at muffin, chorused, 'Dreadful, isn't it! A female authoress!'—this, with a fine disregard of the fact that an authoress is generally a female. 'No doubt steeped in ink and immorality! Poor Carlyon! *My* mother knew *his* father!'

This remark of Mrs. Snooksey's had evidently some profound bearing on the subject, because everybody looked politely impressed, though no one could see where the point came in.

'She's ugly, of course!' tittered Miss Spitely, nervously conscious that once—once, at a ball—Carlyon had picked up her fan, and wishing she had 'gone in' for him then. 'Authoresses always are, aren't they?'

'This one isn't,' put in the One Man, who through some persecuting fate always manages to turn up in a jaded and gloomy condition at these kind of 'afternoon teas.' 'She's pretty. That's the worst of it. Of course she'll lead Carlyon a devil of a life!'

'Of course!' groaned Mrs. Snooksey and Mrs. Tooksey in melancholy duet. 'What else can you expect of a—of a public character? Poor, dear Carlyon! One cannot help feeling sorry for him!'

So on, and in such wise, the jumble of humanity which is called 'society' gabbled, sniggered and sneered; nevertheless, despite dismal head-shakings and dreary forebodings, 'poor, dear Carlyon' carried out his intention, and married Delicia in the presence of one of the most brilliant assemblages of notabilities ever assembled at a wedding. The marriage of a Guards officer is always a pretty sight, but when the fame of Delicia was added to the fame of the regiment, it was no wonder the affair created a sensation and a flutter in the world of fashionable news and ladies' pictorials. Delicia astonished and irritated several members of her own sex by the extreme simplicity of her dress on the occasion. She always managed somehow, quite unintentionally, to astonish and irritate her sweet 'sisters' in womanhood, who, forced to admit her intellectual superiority to themselves, loved her accordingly. Thus her very wedding garment was an affront to them, being only a classic gown of softly-draped white silk *crêpe-de-chine*, without any adornment of either lace or flowers. Then her bridal veil was a vexatious thing, because it was so unusually becoming—it was made of white chiffon, and draped her, like a moonlight mist, from head to foot, a slender chaplet of real orange-blossoms being worn with it. And that was all—no jewels, no bouquet—she only carried a small ivory prayer-book with a plain gold cross mounted on the cover. She looked the very picture of a Greek vestal virgin, but in the eyes of the fashion-plate makers there was a deplorable lack of millinery about her. What would God think of it! Could anything be more irreverent than for a woman of position and fortune to take her marriage-vows before the altar of the Most High without wearing either a court train or diamonds! And the bridesmaids made no great 'show'—they were only little girls, none of them over ten years of age. There were eight of these small damsels, clad in blush-pink like human roses, and very sweet they looked following the lissom, white-veiled form of Delicia as she moved with her own peculiarly graceful step and ethereal air between the admiring rows of the selected men of her husband's regiment, who lined either side of the chancel in honour of the occasion. The ceremony was brief; but those who were present somehow felt it to be singularly impressive. There was a faint suggestion of incongruity in the bridegroom's eloquently-pronounced declaration—'With all my worldly goods I thee endow,' which provoked one of his brother officers to profanely whisper in the ear of a friend, 'By Jove! I don't think he's got anything to give her but his hair-brushes. They were a present; but most of his other things are on tick!'

This young gentleman's unbecoming observations were promptly quashed, and the holy ordinance was concluded to the crashing strains of Mendelssohn. A considerably large crowd, moved by feelings of sincere appreciation for the union of the professions of War and Literature, waited outside the church to give the bride a cheer as she stepped into her carriage, and some of them, hustling a little in advance of the policemen on duty, and peering up towards the entrance of the sacred edifice, were rewarded by seeing the Most Distinguished Personage in the realm, smiling his ever-cordial smile, and shaking hands with the fair 'celebrity' just wedded. At this sight a deafening noise broke out from the throats of the honest 'masses,' a noise which became almost tumultuous when the Distinguished Personage walked by the side of the newly-married pair down the red-carpeted pavement from the church to the nuptial carriage-door, and lifted his hat again and again to the 'huzzas' which greeted him. But the Distinguished Personage did not get all the applause by any means. Delicia got the most of it, and many of the crowd pelted her with flowers which they had brought with them for the purpose. For she was one of the few 'beloved women' that at rare intervals are born to influence nations—so few they are and so precious in their lives and examples that it is little wonder nations make much of them when they find them. There were people in the crowd that day who had wept and smiled over Delicia's writings, and who had, through her teaching, grown better, happier and more humane men and women; and there was a certain loving jealousy in these which grudged that she should stoop from her lofty height of fame, to marry, like any other ordinary woman. They would have had her exempt from the common lot, and yet they all desired her happiness. So in half-gladness, half-regret, they cheered her and threw roses and lilies at her, for it was the month of June; and she with her veil thrown back, and the sunshine glinting on her gold hair, smiled bewitchingly as she bowed right and left to the clamorous throng of her assembled admirers; then, with her glorious six feet of husband, she stepped into her carriage and drove away to the sound of a final cheer. The Distinguished Personage got into his brougham and departed. The brilliantly-attired guests dispersed slowly, and with much chatting and gaiety, in their different directions, and all was over. And the One Man whose earthly lot it was to appear at various 'afternoon teas,' stood under the church portico and muttered gloomily to an acquaintance,—

'Fancy that simple-looking creature being actually the famous Delicia Vaughan! She isn't in the least like an authoress—she's only a woman!' Whereat the acquaintance, whose intellectual resources were somewhat limited, smiled and murmured,—

'Oh, well, when it came to that, you know, you couldn't expect a woman to be anything else, could you? The idea was certainly that authoresses should be—well! a sort of no-sex, ha-ha-ha!—plenty of muscle about them, but scrappy as to figure and doubtful in complexion, with a general air of spectacled wisdom—yes, ha-ha! Well, if it came to that, you know, it must be owned Miss Vaughan—beg her pardon!—Mrs. Carlyon, was not by any means up to the required mark. Ha-ha-ha! Graceful little woman, though; very fascinating—and as for money—whew-w! Beauty Carlyon has fallen on his feet this time, and no mistake! Ha-ha! Good-morning!'

With this, he and the One Man nodded to each other and went in opposite directions. The verger of the church came out, glowered suspiciously at stragglers, picked up a few bridal flowers from the red carpet, and shut the church gates. There had been a wedding, he said condescendingly to one or two nursemaids who had just arrived breathlessly on the scene, wheeling perambulators in front of them, but it was over; the company had gone home. The Distinguished Personage had gone home too. Thus there was nothing to see, and nothing to wait for. Depart, disappointed nursemaids! The vow that binds two in one—that ties Intellect to Folly, Purity to Sensuality, Unselfishness to Egotism—has been taken before the Eternal; and, so far as we can tell, the Eternal has accepted it. There is nothing more to be said or done—the sacrifice is completed.

All this had happened three years ago, yet Delicia, writing peacefully as usual in the quiet seclusion of her study, remembered every incident of her wedding as though it were only yesterday. Happiness had made the time fly on swift wings, and her dream of love had as yet lost nothing of its heavenly glamour. Her marriage had caused no very perceptible change in her fortunes—she worked a little harder and more incessantly, that was all. Her husband deserved all the luxuries and enjoyments of life that she could give him—so she considered—and she was determined he should never have to complain of her lack of energy. Her fame steadily increased—she was at the very head and front of her profession—people came from far and near to have the privilege of seeing her and speaking with her, if only for a few minutes. But popular admiration was nothing to her, and she attached no importance whatever to the daily tributes she received, from all parts of the world, testifying to her genius and the influence her writings had upon the minds of thousands. Such things passed her by as the merest idle wind of rumour, and all her interests were concentrated on her work—first, for the work's own sake, and next, that she might be a continual glory and exhaustless gold mine to her husband.

Certainly Carlyon had nothing to desire or to complain of in his destiny. A crowned king might have envied him; unweighted with care, no debts, no difficulties, a perpetual balance at his banker's, a luxurious home, arranged not only with all the skill that wealth can command, but also with the artistic taste that only brains can supply; a lovely wife whose brilliant endowments were the talk of two continents, and last, but not least, the complete unfettered enjoyment of his own way and will. Delicia never played the domestic tyrant over him; he was free to do as he liked, go where he would and see whom he chose. She never catechised him as to the nature of his occupations or amusements, and he, on his part, was wise enough to draw a line between a certain 'fast set' he personally favoured, and the kind of people he introduced to her, knowing well enough that were he to commit the folly of bringing some 'shady' character within his wife's circle of acquaintance, it would be only once that the presence of such a person would be tolerated by her. For she had very quick perceptions; and though her disposition was gentleness itself, she was firmly planted in rectitude, and managed to withdraw herself so quietly and cleverly from any contact with social swindlers and vulgar *nouveaux riches*, that they never had the ghost of a chance to gain the smallest footing with her. Unable to obtain admittance to her house, they took refuge in scandal, and invented lies and slanders concerning her, all of which fell flat owing to her frankly open life of domestic peace and contentment. Sneers and false rumours were inserted about her in the journals; she ignored them, and quietly lived them down, till finally the worst thing anyone could find to say of her was that she was 'idiotically in love' with her own husband.

'She's a perfect fool about him!' exclaimed the Tookseys and Snookseys, angrily. 'Everybody knows Paul Valdis is madly in love with her. It's only she who never seems to see it!' 'Perhaps she does not approve of the French fashion of having a lover as well as a husband,' suggested a Casual Caller of the male sex. 'Though it is now *la mode* in England, she may not like it. Besides, Paul Valdis has been "madly in love," as you call it, a great many times!'

The Tookseys and Snookseys sighed, shivered, rolled up their eyes and shrugged their shoulders. They were old and ugly and yellow of skin; but their hearts had a few lively pulsations of evil left in them still, and they envied and marvelled at the luck of a woman—a literary female, too, good heavens! to think of it!—who not only had the handsomest man in town for a husband, but who could also have the next handsomest—Paul Valdis, the great actor—for a lover, if she but 'dropped the handkerchief.'

And while 'society' thus talked, Delicia worked, coining money for her husband to spend as he listed. She reserved her household expenses, and took a moderate share of her earnings for her own dress, but all the rest was his. He drove 'tandem' in the Row with two of the most superb horses ever seen in that fashionable thoroughfare. In the early spring mornings he was seen cantering up and down on a magnificent Arab, which for breed and action was the envy of princes. He had his own four-in-hand coach, which he drove to Ranelagh, Hurlingham, and the various race meetings of the year, with a party of 'select' people on top—the kind of 'select' whom Delicia never knew or cared to know, consisting of actresses, betting men, 'swells about town,' and a sprinkling of titled dames, who had frankly thrown over their husbands in order to drink brandy privately, and play the female Don Juan publicly. Occasionally a 'candid friend,' moved by a laudable desire to make mischief between husband and wife, would arrive, full-armed at all points with gossip, and would casually remark to Delicia,—

'Oh, by the way, I saw your husband at Ranelagh the other day with—well!—some *rather* odd people!' To which Delicia would reply tranquilly, 'Did you? I hope he was amusing himself.' Then with a straight, half-disdainful look of her violet eyes at the intruding meddler, she would add, 'I know what you mean, of course! But it is a man's privilege to entertain himself in his own fashion, even with "odd" people if he likes. "Odd" people are always infinitely diverting, owing to their never being able to recognise their own abnormal absurdity. And I never play spy on my husband. I consider a wife who condescends to become a detective as the most contemptible of creatures living.'

Whereupon the 'candid friend,' vexed and baffled, would retire behind an entrenchment of generalities, and afterwards, at 'afternoons' and social gatherings, would publicly opine that, 'It was most probable Mrs. Carlyon was carrying on a little game of her own, as she seemed so indifferent to her husband's goings-on. She was a deep one, oh, yes! very deep! She knew a thing or two!—and perhaps, who could tell?—Paul Valdis had his own reasons for specially "fixing" her with his dark, passionate eyes whenever she appeared in her box at the theatre where he was playing the chief character in an English version of "Ernani."

It was true enough that Delicia was hardly ever seen at the places her husband most frequented, but this happened because he was fond of racing and she was not. She disliked the senseless, selfish and avaricious side of life so glaringly presented at the favourite 'turf' resorts of the 'swagger' set, and said so openly.

'It makes me think badly of everybody,' she declared once to her husband, when he had languidly suggested her 'turning up' at the Oaks. 'I begin to wonder what was the use of Christ dying on the cross to redeem such greedy, foolish folk. I don't want to despise my fellow-creatures, but I'm obliged to do it when I go to a race. So it's better I should stay at home and write, and try to think of them all as well as I can.'

And she did stay at home very contentedly; and when he was absent with a party of his own particular 'friends,' dispensing to them the elegant luncheon and champagne which her work had paid for, she was either busy with some fresh piece of literary labour, or else taking her sweet presence into the houses of the poor and suffering, and bringing relief, hope and cheerfulness, wherever she went. And on the morning when the sunshine placed a crown on her head, and hurled a javelin of light full in the cold eyes of the marble Antinous, she was in one of her brightest, most radiant moods, satisfied with her lot, grateful for the blessings which she considered were so numerous, and as unconscious as ever that there was anything upside down in the arrangement which had resulted in her being obliged to 'love, honour, obey,' keep, and clothe, six feet of beautiful man, by her own unassisted toil, while the said six feet of beautiful man did nothing but enjoy himself.

The quaint 'Empire' clock, shaped as a world, with a little god of love pointing to the hours numbered on its surface, chimed two from its golden bracket on the wall before she laid down her pen for the day. Then, rising, she stretched her fair, rounded arms above her head, and smiled at the daffodils in the vase close by—bright flowers which seemed fully conscious of the sunshine in that smile. Anon, she moved into the deep embrasure of her wide lattice window, where, stretched out at full length, lay a huge dog of the St. Bernard breed, winking lazily with one honest brown eye at the sunbeams that danced about him.

'Oh, Spartan, you lazy fellow!' she said, putting her small foot on his rough, brown body, 'aren't you ashamed of yourself?'

Spartan sighed, and considered the question for a moment, then raised his noble head and kissed the point of his mistress's broidered shoe.

'It's lunch-time, Spartan,' continued Delicia, stooping down to pat him tenderly. 'Will master be home to luncheon, or not, Spartan? I'm afraid not, old boy. What do you think about it?'

This inquiry roused Spartan to an attitude of attention. He got up, sat on his big haunches, and yawned profoundly; then he appeared to meditate, conveying into his fine physiognomy an expression of deep calculation that was almost human.

'No, Spartan,' went on Delicia, dropping on one knee and putting her arm round him, 'we mustn't expect it. We generally lunch alone, and we'll go and get what the gods have provided for us in the dining-room, at once—shall we?'

But Spartan suddenly pricked his long ears, and rose in all his lion-like majesty, erect on his four handsome legs; then he gave one deep

MARIE CORELLI

bark, turning his eyes deferentially on his mistress as one who should say, 'Excuse me, but I hear something which compels my attention.'

Delicia, her hand on the dog's neck, listened intently; her breath came and went, then she smiled, and a lovely light irradiated her face as the velvet *portière* of her study door was hastily pushed aside, and her husband, looking the very incarnation of manly beauty in his becoming riding-gear, entered abruptly.

'Why, Will, how delightful!' she exclaimed, advancing to meet him, 'you hardly ever come home to lunch. This is a treat!'

She clung to him and kissed him. He held her round the waist a moment, gazing at her with the involuntary admiration her grace and intelligence always roused in him, and thinking for the hundredth time how curious it was that she should be so entirely different to other women. Then, releasing her, he drew off his gloves, threw them down, and glanced at the papers which strewed her writing-table.

'Finished the book?' he queried, with a smile.

'Yes, all but the last few sentences,' she replied. 'They require careful thinking out. It doesn't do to end with a platitude.'

'Most books end so,' he said carelessly. 'But yours are always exceptions to the rule. People are never tired of asking me how you do it. One fellow to-day said he was sure I helped you to write the strong parts.'

Delicia smiled a little.

'And what did you say?'

'Why, of course I said I didn't—couldn't write a line to save my life!' he responded, with a laugh. 'But you know what men are! They never can bring themselves to believe in the reality of a woman's genius.'

The musing smile still lingered on Delicia's face.

'Genius is a big thing,' she said. 'I do not assume to possess it. But it is curious to see how very many quite ungifted men announce their own claims to it, while indignantly denying all possibility of its endowment to women. However, one must have patience; it will take some time to break men of their old savagery. For centuries they treated women as slaves and cattle; it may take other centuries before they learn to treat them as their equals.'

Carlyon looked at her, half-wonderingly, half-doubtfully.

'They won't give them full academic honours yet,' he said, 'which I think is disgracefully unfair. And the Government won't give them titles of honour in their own right for their services in Science, Art or Literature, which they ought to have, in my opinion. And this brings me round to the news which sent me galloping home to-day as soon as I heard it. Delicia, I can give you a title this morning!'

She raised her eyebrows a little.

'Are you joking, Will?'

'Not a bit of it. You've heard me speak of my brother Guy, Lord Carlyon?'

She nodded.

'Well, when my father died a bankrupt, of course Guy had what he could get out of the general wreck, which was very little, together with the title. The title was no use to him, he having no means to keep it up. He went off to Africa, gold-hunting, under an assumed name, to try and make money out there—and—and now he's dead of fever. I can't pretend to be very sorry, for I never saw much of him after we left school, and he was my senior by five years. Anyhow, he's gone—and so—in fact—I'm Lord Carlyon!'

He made such a whimsical attempt to appear indifferent to the honour of being a lord, while all the time it was evident he was swelling with the importance of it, that Delicia laughed outright, and her violet eyes flashed with fun as she dropped him a demure curtsey.

'My lord, allow me to congratulate your lordship!' she said. 'By my halidame, good my lord, I am your lordship's very humble servant!'

He looked a trifle vexed.

'Don't be nonsensical, Delicia!' he urged. 'You know I never expected it. I always thought Guy would have married. If he had, and a son had been born to him, of course that son would have had the title. But he remained a bachelor to the end of his days, and so the luck has fallen to me. Aren't you rather pleased about it? It's a nice thing for you, at anyrate.'

Delicia gave him a bright glance of humorous surprise.

'A nice thing for me? My dear boy, do you really think so? Do you really and truly imagine I care about a title tacked on to my name? Not a bit of it! It will only attract a few extra snobs round me at parties, that's all. And to my public I am always Delicia Vaughan; they won't even give me the benefit of *your* name, Will, because somehow they prefer the one by which they knew and loved me first.'

A faint suggestion of the Beautiful Sullenness manner clouded Carlyon's face.

'Oh, of course, you swear by your public!' he said, a trifle crossly. 'But whatever you may think of it, I'm glad the title has come my way. It's a good thing—it gives me a *status*.'

She was silent, and stood quietly beside him, stroking Spartan's head. Not a thought of the *status* she herself gave her husband by her world-wide fame crossed her mind, and the reproach that might have leaped to the lips of a less loving woman than she was—namely, that the position she had won by her own brilliant intellect far outweighed any trumpery title of heritage—never once occurred to her brain. But all the same, something in the composed grace of her attitude conveyed the impression of that fact to Carlyon silently, and with subtle force; for he was conscious of a sudden sense of smallness and inward shame.

'Yet after all,' she said presently, with a playful air, 'it isn't as if you were a brewer, you know! So many brewers and building contractors become lords nowadays, that somehow I always connect the peerage with Beer and Bricks. I suppose it's very wrong, but I can't help it. And it will seem odd to me at first to associate you with the two B's—you are so different to the usual type.'

He smiled,—well pleased to see her eyes resting upon him with the tender admiration to which he had become accustomed.

'Is luncheon ready?' he asked, after a brief pause, during which he was satisfied that he looked his best and that she was fully aware of it.

'Yes; let us go down and partake thereof,' she answered gaily. 'Will you tell the servants, or shall I?'

'Tell the servants what?' he demanded, with a slight frown.

She turned her pretty head over her shoulder laughingly.

'Why, to call you for the future "My Lord," or "m'lud." Which shall it be?'

She looked charmingly provocative; his momentary ill-humour passed, and he flung an arm round her waist and kissed her.

'Whichever you please,' he said. 'Anyway you are, as you always have been, "my" lady!'

II

Delicia was perfectly right when she said that her new distinction would draw 'extra snobs' around her. A handle to one's name invariably attracts all the social 'runaways,'—in the same fashion that mischievous street-boys are attracted to bang at a particularly ornate and glittering door-knocker and then scamper off in hiding before any servant has time to answer the false summons. People who are of old and good family themselves think nothing of titles, but those who have neither good birth, breeding nor education, attach a vast amount of importance to these placards of rank, and can never refrain from an awe-stricken expression of countenance when introduced to a duke, or with-hold the regulation 'royalty-dip' when in the presence of some foreign 'princess,' who, as a matter of fact, has no right to 'royalty' honours at all. Delicia had met a great many such small dignitaries, but she never curtsied to any of them, whereat their petty vanity was wounded, and they thought, 'These authors have bad manners.' She read their thoughts and smiled, but did not care. She reserved her salutations for Royalty itself, not for the imitation of it. And now that she was a 'ladyship,' she obtained a good deal of amusement out of the study of character among her various 'friends' who envied and grudged her the trumpery honour. The Tookseys and Snookseys of society could scarcely contain themselves for spite when they learned that for the future they would have to speak of the 'female authoress' as Lady Carlyon. The Casual Caller and the One Man began to allude to her as 'Delicia, Lady Carlyon,' rolling the sweet, quaint name of 'Delicia' on their tongues with a keener sense of enjoyment than usual in its delicate flavour, thereby driving the Tookseys and Snookseys into a more feverish condition then ever. Paul Valdis heard the news suddenly, when he was dressing for his part as Ernani, on an evening when Royalty had announced its 'gracious' intention of being present to see him do it. And there would appear to have been something not altogether incorrect in the rumour that he was 'madly in love' with Delicia, for he turned very white and lost command of his usual equable temper in an altercation with his 'dresser,' whom he dismissed abruptly with something like an oath.

"'Lady' Carlyon!" he said to himself, staring at his own classic face and brilliant, dark eyes in the little mirror which dominated his 'make-up' table. 'And I no more than mime!—stage-puppet and plaything of the public! Wait, though! I am something more! I am a MAN!—in heart and soul and feeling! a man, which my "Lord" Carlyon is not!'

And he played that night, not for Royalty, which clapped its lavender kid gloves at him in as much enthusiastic approval as Royalty ever shows, but for her new 'ladyship,' who sat in a box overlooking the stage, dressed in pure white with a knot of lilies at her bosom, dreamily unconscious that Ernani was anything but Ernani, or that Valdis was putting his own fiery soul into Victor Hugo's dummy, and making it live, breathe and burn with a passionate ardour never equalled on the stage, and of which she, Delicia, was the chief inspiration.

Delicia was, in very truth, curiously unconscious of the excitement and unrest she always managed to create around herself unintentionally. Her strong individuality was to blame, but she was as unaware of the singular influence she exerted as a rose is unaware of the fragrance its sheds. Everything she did was watched and commented upon—her manners, her dress, her gestures, the very turn of her head, and the slow, supple movements of her body. And society was for ever on the lookout for a glance, a sigh, a word which might indicate the 'dropping of the handkerchief' to Paul Valdis. But the closest espionage failed to discover anything compromising in Delicia's way of life or daily conduct. This caused the fury of the Tookseys and Snookseys to rage unabatedly, while, so far as Delicia herself was concerned, she had no thought beyond the usual two subjects which absorbed her existence— her work and her husband. Her title made no sort of difference to her in herself—'Delicia Vaughan' was still the charmed name wherewith she 'drew' her public, many of whom scarcely glanced at the 'Lady Carlyon' printed in small type between brackets, underneath the more famous appellation on the title-pages of all her books. And in her own mind she was more amused than edified by the flunkey-like attention shown to her 'ladyship' honours.

'How nice for you,' said a female acquaintance to her on one of her visiting days, 'to have a title! Such a distinction for literature, isn't it?'

'Not at all!' answered Delicia, tranquilly, 'It is a distinction for the title to have literature attached to it!'

The female acquaintance started violently.

'Dear me!' and she tittered; 'You really—er—excuse me! seem to have a very good opinion of yourself!'

Delicia's delicate brows drew together in a proud line.

'You mistake,' she said; 'I have no good opinion of myself at all, but I have of Literature. Perhaps you will more clearly understand what I mean if I remind you that there have been several Lord Byrons, but Literature makes it impossible to universally recognise more than one. Literature can add honour to the peerage, but the peerage can never add honour to Literature—not, at any rate, to what *I* understand as Literature.'

'And what is your definition of Literature, Lady Carlyon, may I ask?' inquired a deferential listener to the conversation.

'Power!' replied Delicia, closing her small, white hand slowly and firmly, as though she held the sceptre of an empire in its grasp. 'The power to make men and women think, hope and achieve; the power to draw tears from the eyes, smiles from the lips of thousands; the power to make tyrants tremble, and unseat false judges in authority; the power to strip hypocrisy of its seeming fair disguise, and to brand liars with their name writ large for all the world to see!'

The female acquaintance got up, disturbed in her mind. She did not like the look of Delicia's violet eyes which flashed like straight shafts of light deep into the dark recesses of her soul.

'I must be going,' she murmured. 'So sorry! It's quite delightful to hear you talk, Lady Carlyon, you are so very eloquent!—but I have another call to make—he-he-he!—good afternoon!'

But the Deferential Listener lingered, strangely moved.

'I wish there were more writers who felt as you do, Lady Carlyon!' he said gently. 'I knew you first as Delicia Vaughan, and loved your books—'

'I hope you will try and love them still,' she said simply. 'There is no difference, I assure you, between Delicia Vaughan and Lady Carlyon; they are, and always will be, the same working woman!'

She gave him her hand in parting; he stooped low, kissed it and went. Left alone with the great dog, Spartan, she sat looking musingly up at the glossy, spreading leaves of the giant palm that towered up to the ceiling from a painted Sèvres vase in the middle of her drawing-room, and almost for the first time in her life a faint shadow of trouble and uneasiness clouded her bright nature.

'How I do hate humbug!' she thought. 'It seems to me that I have had to put up with so much more of it lately than I ever had before; it's this wretched title, I suppose. I wish I could dispense with it altogether; it does not please me, though it pleases Will. He is so good-natured that he does not seem able to distinguish between friends, and others who are mere toadies. It would be a good thing for me if I had the same unsuspecting disposition; but, most unfortunately, I see things as they are—not as they appear to be.'

And this was true. She did see things clearly and comprehensively always;—except in one direction. There she was totally blind. But in her blindness lay all her happiness, and though the rose-coloured veil of illusion was wearing thin, no rent had yet been made in it.

It was her 'at home' day, and she sat waiting resignedly for the callers who usually flocked to her between five and six in the afternoon. The two people who had come and gone, namely, the Female Acquaintance and the Deferential Listener, had been chance visitors out of the ordinary run. And it was only half-past four when a loud ring at the bell made Spartan growl and look to his mistress for orders to bite, if necessary.

'Quiet, Spartan!' said Delicia, gently. 'We are "at home" to-day, you know! You mustn't bark at anybody.'

Spartan rolled his eyes discontentedly. He hated 'at home' days, and he went off in a far corner of the drawing-room, where there was a convenient bear-skin rug to lie on; there he curled himself up to sleep. Meanwhile the visitor who had rung the bell so violently was announced—'Mrs. Lefroy,'—and Delicia rose, with a slightly weary and vexed air, as a handsome woman, over-dressed and over-powdered, entered the room; her white teeth bared to view in the English 'society smile.'

'My dear!' she exclaimed, 'how delightful you look, and what a perfectly lovely room! I have seen it often before, of course, and yet it seems to me always lovelier! And you, too!—what a *sweet* gown! Oh, my dear, I have such fun to tell you; I know you didn't expect to see me! I got away from the Riviera much sooner than I thought I should. All my money went at Monte Carlo in the most frightfully rapid way, and so I came back to town—one can have larks in town as well as anywhere else, without the temptation of that dear, wicked, fascinating Casino! And, my dear, nothing is talked of but your book; everybody's waiting for it with the greatest impatience—it's finished, isn't it? In the hands of the publishers! How delightful! And, of course, you have got loads of money for it? How nice for you, and for that glorious-looking husband of yours! And you are looking so well! No tea, dearest, thank you! Oh, I really must take off my cloak a moment—thanks! Is there anyone else coming to-day? Oh, of course, you always have *crowds*! That is why I want to tell you what fun we had last night; Lord Carlyon never expected we should see him, you know!'

Delicia looked up from the tea tray whither she had moved on the impulse of hospitality. She had not spoken; she knew Mrs. Lefroy of old, and was aware that it was better to let her have her talk out.

'Of course,' went on Mrs. Lefroy, 'you have heard of Marina, the new dancer—the girl who appears on the stage like a hooded cobra, and gradually winds herself out of her serpent-skin into a woman with scarcely any clothes on, and dances about among a lot of little snakes of fire, done with electricity? The one that all the men are going mad over, on account of her wonderful legs?'

Delicia, with a slight movement, more of regret than offence, nodded.

'Well, we were having supper at the Savoy last night, and what do you think, my dear!' And here Mrs. Lefroy clasped her well-gloved hands together in a kind of slander-mongering ecstasy. 'Who should come in and sit down at the very next table, but Lord Carlyon and this very Marina!'

Delicia turned round slowly, her eyes shining, and a smile on her mouth.

'Well?' she said.

Mrs. Lefroy's nose reddened through the powder, and she tossed her head.

'Well? Is that all you say—well? I should certainly find some more forcible observation than that, if I heard of *my* husband taking the Marina to supper at the Savoy!'

'Would you?' said Delicia, smiling. 'But then, you see, I am not you, and your husband is not my husband. There's all the difference! Besides, men are free to amuse themselves in their own way, provided they wrong no one by doing so.'

'With "creatures" like Marina?' inquired Mrs. Lefroy, with a wide smile. 'Really, my dear, you are extremely tolerant! Do you know that even Paul Valdis, an actor—and you wouldn't think he was particular— would not be seen with the Cobra person!'

'Mr. Valdis chooses his own associates, no doubt, to please his own taste,' said Delicia, quietly. 'It is nothing to me whether he would be seen with the Cobra person, as you call her, or whether he would not. If my husband likes to talk to her, there must be something clever about her, and something nice, too, I should imagine. All dancers are not demons.'

'My poor Delicia!' exclaimed Mrs. Lefroy. 'Really, you are too unsuspicious and sweet for anything! If you would only let me open your eyes a little—'

'The Duke and Duchess of Mortlands,' announced the maid-in-waiting at this juncture; and the conversation was broken off for the reception of a very stately old lady and a very jolly old gentleman. The old gentleman took a cup of tea, and bowed so often to Delicia over it that he spilt some drops of tea down his waistcoat, while his portly spouse spread cake-crumbs profusely over the broad expanse known to dressmakers and tailors as the 'bust measurement.' They were charming old people, though untidy; and being of an immensely ancient family, their ancestors having had something to do with the Battle of Crecy, they admired Delicia for herself and her brilliant gifts alone, even to the forgetting of her married name occasionally, and to the calling of her 'Miss Vaughan,' for which slip they instantly apologised. Numbers of people now began to arrive, and Delicia's drawing-rooms were soon full. A famous Swedish cantatrice came among others, and in her own pleasant way offered to sing a 'Mountain Melody' of her native land. Her rich voice was still pealing through the air when there was a slight stir and excitement among the silent listeners to the music, and Paul Valdis entered unannounced. He stood near the door till the song that was being sung had ended, then he advanced towards Delicia, who greeted him with her usual simple grace, and showed no more effusion towards him than she had shown to the old duke who had spilt his tea. He was pale and somewhat absent-minded; though he talked generalities with several people present, much as he disliked talking generalities. Now and then he became gloomy and curt of speech, and at such moments, Mrs. Lefroy, watching him, felt that she would have given worlds to stay on and hide herself somewhere behind a curtain that she might see how he was going to comport himself after the gabbling crowd had gone. But she had already stayed more than an hour—she would get no more chance of talking to Delicia—she was obliged to go home and dress for a dinner-party that evening; so finally she reluctantly made the best of a bad business, and glided up to her hostess to say good-bye.

'So sorry to be going!' she murmured. 'I really wish I could have a few minutes' private talk with you! But you are such a busy woman!'

'Yes, I am!' agreed Delicia, smiling. 'However, opportunities for talking scandal always turn up sometime or other—don't you find it so?'

Mrs. Lefroy was not quite proof against this delicate home-thrust. She felt distinctly angry. But there was no time to show it. She forced a smile and went—determining within herself that some day she would shake the classic composure of the 'female authoress' to its very foundations, and make of her a trembling, weak, jealous woman like many others whom she knew who were blessed with husbands like Lord Carlyon.

Gradually the 'after-tea' crowd dispersed, and Delicia was left alone with only one remaining visitor—Paul Valdis. The dog Spartan rose from the corner where he had lain peacefully retired from view during the crush of visitors, and advancing majestically, with wagging tail, laid a big head caressingly on the actor's knee. Valdis patted him and spoke out his thought involuntarily.

'One, at least, out of your many friends, is honest, Lady Carlyon,' he said.

Delicia, somewhat fatigued with the business of receiving her guests, had seated herself in a low arm-chair, her head leaning back on a cushion, and now she looked round, slightly smiling. 'You mean Spartan?' she said, 'or yourself?'

'I mean Spartan,' he replied, with a touch of passion; 'A dog may be honest without offence to the world in general, but a man must never be honest, unless he wishes to be considered a fool or a madman, or both.'

She regarded him intently for a moment. Her artistic eye quickly took note of the attractive points of his face and figure, and, with the perception of a student of character, she appreciated the firm and manly lines of the well-shaped hand that rested on Spartan's head, but it was with the admiration which she would have given to a fine picture more readily than to a living being. Something, however, troubled her as she looked, for she saw that he was suppressing some strong emotion in her presence, and her first thought was that the English version of 'Ernani' was going to prove a failure.

'You speak bitterly, Mr. Valdis,' she said, after a pause, 'and yet you ought not to do so, considering the brilliancy of your position and your immense popularity.'

'Does a brilliant position and immense popularity satisfy a man, do you think?' he asked, not looking at her, but keeping his gaze on the honest brown eyes of Spartan, who, with the quaint conceit of a handsome dog who knows his own value, went on wagging his tail,

MARIE CORELLI

under the impression that the conversation was addressed to him alone. 'Though I suppose it ought to satisfy an actor, who, by some folks, is considered hardly a man at all. But if we talk of position and popularity, you far outbalance me in honours—and are you satisfied?'

'Perfectly!' and Delicia smiled full into his eyes; 'I should, indeed, be ungrateful if I were not.'

He made a slight movement of impatience.

'Ungrateful! How strange that word sounds from your lips! Why use it at all? You are surely the last person on earth who should speak of gratitude, for you owe no one anything. You have worked for your fame,—worked harder than anyone I know,—and you have won it; you have given out the treasures of your genius to the public, and they reward you by their love and honour; it is a natural sequence of cause and effect. There is no reason why you should be grateful for what is merely the just recognition of your worth.'

'You think not?' said Delicia, still smiling. 'Ah, but I cannot quite agree with you! You see there have been so many who have toiled for fame and never won it,—so many who have poured out the "treasures of their genius," to quote your own words, on a totally unappreciative world which has never recognised them till long after they are dead. And that is why I consider one cannot be too grateful for a little kindness from one's fellow-creatures while one is living; though, if you ask the Press people, they will tell you it's a very bad sign of your quality as an author if you succeed. The only proofs of true genius are, never to sell one's books at all, die burdened with debts and difficulties, and leave your name and fame to be glorified by a posterity whom you will never know!'

Valdis laughed; and Delicia, her eyes sparkling with fun, rose from her chair and took up a newspaper from one of the side tables close by.

'Listen!' she said. 'This appears in yesterday's *Morning Chanticleer*, *apropos* of your humble servant—"The rampant lady-novelist, known as Delicia Vaughan, is at it again. Not content with having married 'Beauty' Carlyon of the Guards, who has just stepped into his deceased brother's titled shoes and is now Lord Carlyon, she is about to issue a scathing book on the manners and morals of the present age, written, no doubt, in the usual hysterical style affected by female *poseurs* in literature, whose works appeal chiefly to residents up Brixton and Clapham way. We regret that 'Lady' Carlyon does not see the necessity of 'assuming dignity,' even if she hath it not, on her elevation, through her husband, to the circles of the 'upper ten.'" There, what do you think of that?' she asked gaily, as she flung the journal down.

Valdis had risen, and stood confronting her with frowning brow and flashing eyes. 'Think of it!' he said angrily, 'Why, that I should like to horse-whip the dirty blackguard who wrote it!'

Delicia looked up at him in genuine amazement.

'Dear me!' she exclaimed playfully. 'But why so fierce, friend Ernani? This is nothing—nothing at all to what the papers generally say of me. I don't mind it in the least; it rather amuses me, on the whole.'

'But don't you see how they mistake the position?' exclaimed Valdis, impetuously. 'Don't you see that they are giving your husband all the honour of elevation to the circles of the upper ten; as if you were not there already by the merit of your genius alone! What would Lord Carlyon be without you, even were he twenty times a lord! He owes everything to you, and to your brain-work; he is nothing in himself, and less than nothing! There,—I have gone too far!'

Delicia stood very still; her face was pale, and her beautiful eyes were cold in their shining as the gleam of stars in frosty weather.

'Yes, you have gone too far, Mr. Valdis,' she said, 'and I am sorry—for we were friends.'

She laid the slightest little emphasis on the word 'were,' and the strong heart of the man who loved her sank heavily with a forlorn sense of misery. But the inward rage that consumed him to think that she—the patient, loving woman, who coined wealth by her own unassisted work, while her husband spent the money and amused himself with her earnings—should be publicly sneered at as a nothing, and her worser-half toadied and flattered as if he were a Yankee millionaire in his own right, was stronger than the personal passion he entertained for her, and his manful resentment of the position could not be repressed.

'I am sorry too, Lady Carlyon,' he said hoarsely, avoiding her gaze, 'for I do not feel I can retract anything I have said.'

There was a silence. Delicia was deeply displeased; yet with her displeasure there was mingled a vague sense of uneasiness and fear. She found it difficult to maintain her self-possession; there was something in the defiant look and attitude of Valdis that almost moved her to give way to a sudden, undignified outburst of anger. She was tempted to cry out to him, 'What is it you are hiding from me? There is something—tell me all you know!'

But she bit her lips hard, and laid her hand on Spartan's collar to somewhat conceal its trembling. Thus standing, she bent her head with grave grace and courtesy.

'Good-bye, Mr. Valdis!'

He started, and looked at her half imploringly. The simple words were his dismissal, and he knew it. Because he had, in that unguarded moment, spoken a word in dispraise of the glorious six feet of husband, the doors of Delicia's house would henceforth be closed to him, and the fair presence of Delicia herself would be denied to his sight. It was a blow—but he was a man, and he took his punishment manfully.

'Good-bye, Lady Carlyon,' he said. 'I deserve little consideration at your hands, but I will ask you not to condemn me altogether as a discourteous churl and boor, till—till you know a few things of which you are now happily ignorant. Were I a selfish man, I should wish you to be enlightened speedily concerning these matters; but being, God knows! your true friend'—here his voice trembled—'I pray you may remain a long time yet in the purest paradise known on earth—the paradise of a loving soul's illusion. My hand shall not destroy one blossom in your fairy garden! In old days of chivalry, beautiful and beloved women had champions to defend their honour and renown, and fight for them if needful; and though the old days are no longer with us, chivalry is not quite dead, so that if ever you need a champion—heavens! what am I saying? No wonder you look scornful! Lady Delicia Carlyon to need the championship of an actor! The thing is manifestly absurd! You, in your position, can help me by your influence, but I can do nothing to help you—if by chance you should ever need help. I am talking wildly, and deepening my offences in your eyes; perhaps, however, you will think better of me some day. And so good-bye again—I cannot ask you to forgive me. If ever you desire to see me once more, I will come at your command—but not till then.'

Inflexibly she stood, without offering him her hand in farewell. But he desperately caught that hand, and kissed it with the ardour of an Ernani and Romeo intermingled, then he turned and left the room. Delicia listened to his retreating footsteps as he descended the stairs and passed into the hall below, then she heard the street door close. A great sigh of relief broke from her lips; he was gone,—this impertinent actor who had presumed to say that her husband was 'nothing, and less than nothing'—he was gone, and he would probably never come back. She looked down at Spartan, and found the dog's eyes were turned up to hers in inquiring wonder and sadness. As plainly as any animal could speak by mere expression, he was saying,—

'What is the matter with Valdis? He is a friend of mine, and why have you driven him away?'

'Spartan, dear,' she said, drawing him towards her, 'he is a very conceited man, and he says unkind things about our dear master, and we do not intend to let him come near us any more! These great actors always get spoilt, and think they are lords almighty, and presume to pass judgment on much better men than themselves. Paul Valdis is being so run after and so ridiculously flattered that he will soon become quite unbearable.'

Spartan sighed profoundly; he was not entirely satisfied in his canine mind. He gave one or two longing and wistful glances towards the door, but his wandering thoughts were quickly recalled to his immediate surroundings by the feeling of something warm and wet dropping on his head. It was a tear,—a bright tear, fallen from the beautiful eyes of his mistress,—and in anxious haste he pressed his rough body close against her with a mute caress of inquiring sympathy. In very truth Delicia was crying,—quietly and in a secret way, as though ashamed to acknowledge her emotion even to herself. As a rule, she liked to be able to give a reason for her feelings, but on this occasion she found it impossible to make any analysis of the cause of her tears. Yet they fell fast, and she wiped them away quickly with a little filmy handkerchief as fine as a cobweb, which Spartan, moved by a sudden desire to provide her with some harmless distraction from melancholy, made uncouth attempts to secure as a plaything. He succeeded so far in his clumsy gambols as to bring the flicker of a smile on her face at last, whereat he rejoiced exceedingly, and wagged his tail with a violence that threatened to entirely dislocate that useful member. In a few minutes she was quite herself again, and when her husband returned to dinner, met him with the usual beautiful composure that always distinguished her bearing, though there was an air of thoughtful resolve about her which accentuated the delicate lines of her features and made her look more intellectually classic than ever. When she took her seat at table that evening, her statuesque serenity, combined with her fair face, steadfast eyes, and rich hair knotted loosely at the back of her well-shaped head, gave her so much the aspect of something far superior to the ordinary run of mortal women, that Carlyon, fresh from a game of baccarat, where he had lost over three hundred pounds in a couple of hours, was conscious of a smarting sense of undefinable annoyance.

'I wish you could keep our name out of the papers,' he said suddenly, when dessert was placed before them, and the servants had withdrawn; 'it is most annoying to me to see it constantly cropping up in all manner of vulgar society paragraphs.'

She looked at him steadfastly.

'You used not to mind it so much,' she answered, 'but I am sorry you are vexed. I wish I could remedy the evil, but unfortunately I am quite powerless. When one is a public character, the newspapers will have their fling; it cannot possibly be helped; but if one is leading an honest life in the world, and has no disgraceful secrets to hide, what does it matter after all?'

'I think it matters a great deal,' he grumbled, as he carefully skinned the fine peach on his plate, and commenced to appreciate its flavour. 'I hate to have my movements forestalled and advertised by the Press. And, as far as you are concerned, I am sure I heartily wish you were not a public character.'

She opened her eyes a little.

'Do you? Since when? Since you became Lord Carlyon? My dear boy, if a trumpery little handle to your name is going to make you ashamed of your wife's reputation as an author, I think it's a great pity you ever succeeded to the title.'

'Oh, I know you don't care a bit about it,' he said, keeping his gaze on the juicy peach; 'but other people appreciate it.'

'What other people?' queried Delicia, laughing. 'The droll little units that call themselves "society?" I daresay they do appreciate it—they have got nothing else to think or talk about but "he" and "she" and "we" and "they." And yet poor old Mortlands, who was here this afternoon, forgot all about this same wonderful title many times, and kept on calling me "Miss Vaughan." Then he apologised, and said in extenuation, that to add a "ladyship" to my name was "to gild refined gold and paint the lily." That quotation has often been used before under similar circumstances, but he gave it quite a new flavour of gallantry.'

'The Mortlands family dates back to about the same period as ours,' said Carlyon, musingly.

'As ours? Say as yours, my dear lord!' returned Delicia, gaily, 'for I am sure I do not know where the Vaughans come from. I must go down to the Heralds' College and see if I cannot persuade someone in authority there to pick me out an ancestor who did great deeds before the Carlyons ever existed! Ancestral glory is such a question with you now, Will, that I almost wish I were the daughter of a Chicago pork-packer.'

'Why?' asked Carlyon, a trifle gloomily.

'Why, because I could at any rate get up a past "Pilgrim Father" if necessary. A present-day reputation is evidently not sufficient for you.'

'I think the old days were best,' he said curtly.

'Yes? When the men kept the women within four walls, as cows are kept in byres, and gave them just the amount of food they thought they deserved, and beat them if they were rebellious? Well, perhaps those times were pleasant, but I am afraid I should never have appreciated them. I prefer to see things advancing—as they are—and I like a civilisation which includes the education of women as well as of men.'

'Things are advancing a great deal too quickly, in my opinion,' said Carlyon, languidly, pouring out a glass of the choice claret beside him. 'I should be inclined to vote for a little less rapid progress, in regard to women.'

'Yet only the other day you were saying what a shame it was that women could not win full academic honours like men; and you even said that they ought to be given titles, in reward for their services to Science, Art and Literature,' said Delicia. 'What has made you change your opinion?'

He did not look up at her, but absently played with the crumbs on the table-cloth.

'Well, I am not sure that it is the correct thing for women to appear very prominently in public,' he said.

A momentary contraction of Delicia's fine brows showed that a touch of impatience ruffled her humour. But she restrained herself, and said with perfect composure,—

'I am afraid I don't quite follow your meaning, unless, perhaps, your words apply to the new dancer, La Marina?'

He gave a violent start, and with a sudden movement of his hand upset his wine glass. Delicia watched the red wine staining the satiny whiteness of the damask table-cloth without any exclamation or sign of annoyance. Her heart was beating fast, because through her drooping lashes she saw her husband's face, and read there an expression that was strange and new to her.

'Oh, I know what has happened,' he said fiercely, and with almost an oath, as he strove to wipe off the drops of Chateau Lafite that soiled his cuff as well as the table-cloth. 'That woman Lefroy has been here telling tales and making mischief! I saw her, with her crew of social rowdies, at the Savoy the other night. . .'

'And she saw you!' interpolated Delicia, smiling.

'Well, what if she did?' he snapped out irritably. 'I was introduced to La Marina by Prince Golitzberg—you know that German fellow—and he asked me to take her off his hands. He had promised her a supper at the Savoy, and at the last moment he was sent for to go to his wife, who was seized with sudden illness. I could not refuse to oblige him; he's a decent sort of chap. Then, of course, as luck would have it, in comes that spoil-sport of a Lefroy and makes all this rumpus!'

'My dear Will!' expostulated Delicia, in gentle amazement, 'what are you talking about? Where is the rumpus? What has Mrs. Lefroy done? She simply mentioned to me to-day that she had seen you at the Savoy with this Marina, and there the matter ended, and, as far as I am concerned, there it will for ever end.'

'That is all nonsense!' said Carlyon, still wiping his cuff. 'You know you are put out, or you wouldn't look at me in the way you do!'

Delicia laughed.

'What way am I looking?' she demanded merrily. 'Pray, my dear boy, don't be so conceited as to imagine I mind your taking the Marina, or any amount of Marinas, to supper at the Savoy, if that kind of thing amuses you! Surely you don't suppose that I bring myself into comparison with "ladies" of Marina's class, or that I could be jealous of such persons? I am afraid you do not know me yet, Will, though we have spent such happy years together! You have neither fathomed the depth of my love, nor taken the measure of my pride! Besides,—I trust you!' She paused. Then rising from the table, she handed him the little silver box containing his cigars. 'Smoke off your petulance, dear boy!' she said, 'and join me upstairs when you are ready. We go to the Premier's reception to-night, remember.'

Her hand rested for a moment on his shoulder with a caressing touch; anon, humming a little tune under her breath, and followed by Spartan, who never let her go out of his sight for a moment if he could help it, she left the room. Ascending the staircase, she stopped on the threshold of her study and looked in with a vague air, as though the place had suddenly grown unfamiliar. There, immediately facing her, smiled the pictured lineaments of Shakespeare, that immortal friend of man; her favourite books greeted her with all the silent yet persuasive eloquence of their well-known and deeply-honoured titles; the electric lights, fitted up to represent small stars in the ceiling, were not turned on, and only the young moon peered glimmeringly through the lattice window, shedding a pale lustre on the marble features of the 'Antinous.' Standing quite still, she gazed at all these well-known objects of her daily surroundings with a curious sense of strangeness, Spartan staring up wonderingly at her the while.

'What is it that is wrong with me?' she mused. 'Why do I feel as if I were suddenly thrust out of my usual peace, and made to take a part in the common and mean disputes of petty-minded men and women?'

She waited another minute, then apparently conquering whatever emotion was at work within her, she pressed the ivory handle which diffused light on all visible things, and entered the room with a quiet step and a half-penitent look, as of regret for having given offence to some invisible spirit-monitor.

'Oh, you dear, dear friends!' she said, approaching the bookshelves, and softly apostrophising the volumes ranged there as if they were sentient personages, 'I am afraid I do not consult you half enough! You are always with me, ready to give me the soundest advice on any subject under the sun; advice founded on sage experience, too! Tell me something now, out of your stores of wisdom, to stop this foolish little aching at my heart—this irritating, selfish, suspicious trouble which is quite unworthy of me, as it is unworthy of anyone who has had the high privilege of learning great lessons from such teachers as you are! It is not as if I were a woman whose sole ideas of life are centred on dress and domesticity, or one of those unhappy, self-tormenting creatures who cannot exist without admiration and flattery; I am, I think and hope, differently constituted, and mean to try for great things, even if I never succeed in attaining them. But in trying for greatness, one must not descend to littleness—save me from this danger, my dear old-world comrades, if you can, for to-night I am totally unlike myself. There are thoughts in my brain that might have excited Xantippe, but which should never trouble Delicia, if to herself Delicia prove but true!'

And she raised her eyes, half smiling, to the meditative countenance of Shakespeare. 'Excellent and "divine Williams," you must excuse me for fitting your patriotic line on England to my unworthy needs; but why *would* you make yourself so eminently quotable?' She paused, then took up a book lying on her desk. 'Here is an excellent doctor for a sick, petulant child such as I am—Marcus Aurelius. What will you say to me, wise pagan? Let me see,' and opening a page at random, her eyes fell on the words, 'Do not suppose you are hurt, and your complaint ceases. Cease your complaint and you are not hurt.'

She laughed, and her face began to light up with all its usual animation.

'Excellent Emperor! What a wholesome thrashing you give me! Anything more?' And she turned over a few pages, and came upon one of the imperial moralist's most coolly-dictatorial assertions. 'What an easy matter it is to stem the current of your imagination, to discharge a troublesome or improper thought, and at once return to a state of calm!'

'I don't know about that, Marcus,' she said. 'It is not exactly an "easy" matter to stem the current of imagination, but certainly it's worth trying;' and she read on, 'To-day I rushed clear out of misfortune, or rather, I threw misfortune from me; for, to speak the truth, it was not outside, and never came any nearer than my own fancy.'

She closed the book smilingly—the beautiful equanimity of her disposition was completely restored. She left her pretty writing den, bidding Spartan remain there on guard—a mandate he was accustomed to, and which he obeyed instantly, though with a deep sigh, his mistress's 'evenings out' being the chief trouble of his otherwise enviable existence. Delicia, meantime, went to dress for the Premier's reception, and soon slipped into the robe she had had designed for herself by a famous firm of Indian embroiderers;—a garment of softest white satin, adorned with gold and silver thread, and pearls thickly intertwined, so as to present the appearance of a mass of finely-wrought jewels. A single star of diamonds glittered in her hair, and she carried a fan of natural lilies, tied with white ribbon. Thus attired, she joined her husband, who stood ready and waiting for her in the drawing-room. He glanced up at her somewhat shamefacedly.

'You look your very best this evening, Delicia,' he said.

She made him a sweeping curtsey, and smiled.

'My lord, your favouring praise doth overwhelm me!' she answered. 'Is it not meet and right that I should so appear as to be deemed worthy of the house of Carlyon!

He put his arm round her waist and drew her to him. It was curious, he thought, how fresh her beauty seemed! And how the men in his 'set' would have burst into a loud guffaw of coarse laughter if any of them had thought that such was his opinion of his wife's charm—his own wife, to whom he had been fast wedded for over three years! According to the rules of 'modern' morality, one ought in three years to have had enough of one's lawful wife, and find a suitable 'soul' wherewith to claim 'affinity.'

'Delicia,' he said, playing idly with the lilies of her fan, 'I am sorry you were vexed about the Marina woman—'

She interrupted him by laying her little white-gloved fingers on his lips.

'Vexed? Oh, no, Will, not vexed. Why should I be? Pray don't let us talk about it any more; I have almost forgotten the incident. Come! It's time we started!'

And in response to the oddly penitent, half-sullen manner of the 'naughty boy' he chose to assume, she kissed him. Whereupon he tried that one special method of his, which had given him the victory in his wooing of her, the Passionate Outbreak; and murmuring in his rich voice that she was always the 'one woman in the world,' the 'angel of his life,' and altogether the very crown and summit of sweet perfection, he folded her in his arms with all a lover's fervour. And she, clinging to him, forgot her doubts and fears, forgot the austere observations of Marcus Aurelius, forgot the triumphs of her own intellectual career, forgot everything, in fact, but that she was the blindly-adoring devotee of a six-foot Guardsman, whom she had herself set up as a 'god' on the throne of the Ideal, and whom she worshipped through such a roseate cloud of sweet self-abnegation that she was unable to perceive how poor a fetish her idol was after all—made of nothing but the very commonest clay!

III

The smoking-room of the 'Bohemian' was full of a motley collection of men of the literary vagabond type—reporters, paragraphists, writers of penny dreadfuls, reeled off tape-wise from the thin spools of smoke-dried masculine brains; stray actors, playwrights anxious to translate the work of some famous foreigner and so get fastened on to his superior coat-tails, 'adapters' desirous of dramatising some celebrated novel and pocketing all the profits, anxious 'proposers' of new magazines looking about for 'funds' to back them up, and among all these an extremely casual sprinkling of the brilliant and successful workers in art and literature, who were either honorary members, or who had allowed their names to stand on the committee in order to give 'prestige' to a collection which would otherwise be termed the 'rag-tag and bob-tail' of literature. The opinions of the 'Bohemian,'—the airily idiotic theories with which the members disported themselves, and furnished food for laughter to the profane—were occasionally quoted in the newspapers, which of course gave the club a certain amount of importance in its own eyes, if in nobody else's. And the committee put on what is called a considerable amount of 'side'; now and then affecting to honour some half-and-half celebrity by asking him to a Five-Shilling dinner, and dubbing him the 'guest of the evening,' he meantime gloomily taking note of the half-cold, badly-cooked poorness of the meal, and debating within himself whether it would be possible to get away in time to have a chop 'from the grill' somewhere on his way home. The 'Bohemian' had been a long time getting started, owing to the manner in which the gentlemen who were 'in' persistently black-balled every new aspirant for the honours of membership. The cause of this arose from the chronic state of nervous jealousy in which the 'Bohemians' lived. To a certain extent, and as far as their personal animosities would permit, they were a 'Mutual Admiration Society,' and dreaded the intrusion of any stranger who might set himself to discover 'their tricks and their manners.' They had a lawyer of their own, whose business it was to arrange the disputes of the club, should occasion require his services, and they also had a doctor, a humorous and very clever little man, who was fond of strolling about the premises in the evening, and taking notes for the writing of a medical treatise to be entitled 'Literary Dyspepsia, and the Passion of Envy considered in its

Action on the Spleen and Other Vital Organs,' a book which he justly considered would excite a great deal of interest among his professional compeers. But in spite of the imposing Committee of Names, the lawyer and the doctor, the 'Bohemian' did not pay. It struggled on, hampered with debts and difficulties, like most of its members. It gave smoking-concerts occasionally, for which it charged extra, and twice a year it admitted ladies to its dinners, during which banquets speeches were made distinctly proving to the fair sex that they had no business at all to be present. Still, with every advantage that a running fire of satirical comment could give it in the way of notoriety, the 'Bohemian' was not a prosperous concern; and no Yankee Bullion-Bag seemed inclined to take it up or invest in the chances of its future. A more sallow, sour, discontented set of men than were congregated in the smoking-room on the particular evening now in question could hardly be found anywhere between London and the Antipodes, and only the little doctor, leaning back in a lounge-chair with his neatly-shaped little legs easily crossed, and a smile on his face, seemed to enjoy his position as an impartial spectator of the scene. His smile, however, was one of purely professional satisfaction; he was making studies of a 'subject' in the person of a long-haired 'poet,' who wrote his own reviews. This son of the Muses was an untidy, dirty-looking man, and his abundant locks irresistibly reminded one of a black goat-skin door-mat, worn in places where reckless visitors had wiped their muddy boots thereon. No doubt this poet washed occasionally, but his skin was somewhat of the peculiar composition complained of by Lady Macbeth—'All the perfumes of Arabia' would neither cleanse nor 'sweeten' it.

'Jaundice,' murmured the little doctor, pleasantly; 'I'll give him a year, and he'll be down with its worst form. Too much smoke, too much whisky, combined mentally with conceit, spite, and the habitual concentration of the imagination on self; and no gaiety, wit or kindness to temper the mixture. All bad for the health—as bad as bad can be! But, God bless my soul, what does it matter? He'd never be missed!'

And he rubbed his hands jubilantly, smiling still.

Meanwhile the rhymester thus doomed was seated at a distant table and writing of himself thus,—

'If Shelley was a poet, if Byron was a poet, if we own Shakespeare as a king of bards and dramatists, then Mr. Aubrey Grovelyn is a poet also, eminently fitted to be the comrade of these immortals. Inspired thought, beauty of diction, ease and splendour of rhythm distinguish

Aubrey Grovelyn's muse as they distinguish Shakespeare's utterances; and in bestowing upon this gifted singer the praise that is justly due to him, we feel we are rendering a service to England in being among the first to point out the glorious promise and value of a genius who is destined to outsoar all his contemporaries in far-reaching originality and grandeur of design.'

Finishing this with a bold dash, he put it in an envelope and addressed it to the office of the journal on which he was employed and known, simply as Alfred Brown. Mr. Alfred Brown was on the staff of that journal as a critic; and as Brown he praised himself in the person of Aubrey Grovelyn. The great editor of the journal, being half his time away shooting, golfing, or otherwise amusing himself, didn't know anything about either Grovelyn or Brown, and didn't care. And the public, seeing Grovelyn described as a Shakespeare, promptly concluded he must be a humbug, and avoided his books as cautiously as though they had been labelled 'Poison.' Hence Brown-Aubrey-Grovelyn's chronic yellow melancholy—his poems wouldn't 'sell.' He crammed his eulogistic review of his own latest production into his pocket, and went over to the doctor, from whose cigar he kindled his own.

'Have you seen the papers this evening?' he asked languidly, dropping into a chair next to the club's 'Galen,' and running one skinny hand through his door-mat curls.

'I have just glanced through them,' replied the doctor, indifferently. 'I never do read anything but the telegrams.'

The poet raised his eyebrows superciliously.

'So? You don't allow your mind to be influenced by the ebb and flow of the human tide of events,' he murmured vaguely. 'But I should have thought you would have observed the ridiculous announcement concerning the new book by that horrid woman, Delicia Vaughan. It is monstrous! A sale of one hundred thousand copies; it's an infernal lie!'

'It's a damnation truth!' said a pleasant voice, suddenly, in the mildest of accents; and a good-looking man with a pretty trick of twirling his moustache, and an uncomfortable way of flashing his eyes, squared himself upright in front of both physician and poet. 'I'm the publisher, and I know!'

There was a silence, during which Mr. Grovelyn smiled angrily and re-arranged his door-mat. 'When,' proceeded the publisher, sweetly, 'will you enable me to do the same thing for you, Mr. Grovelyn?'

The doctor, whose name was Dalley, laughed; the poet frowned.

'Sir,' said Grovelyn, 'my work does not appeal to this age, which is merely prolific in the generating of idiots; I trust myself and my productions to the justice of posterity.'

'Then you must appeal to posterity's publishers as well, mustn't he, Mr. Granton?' suggested Doctor Dalley, with a humorous twinkle in his eyes, addressing the publisher, who, being the head of a wealthy and influential firm, was regarded by all the penniless scribblers in the 'Bohemian' with feelings divided betwixt awe and fear.

'He must, indeed!' said Granton. 'Personally, I prefer to speculate in Delicia Vaughan, now Lady Carlyon. Her new book is a masterpiece; I am proud to be the publisher of it. And upon my word, I think the public show capital taste in "rushing" for it.'

'Pooh, she can't write!' sneered Grovelyn. 'Did you ever know a woman who could?'

'I have heard of George Eliot,' hinted Dalley.

'An old hen, that imagined it could crow!' said the poet, with intense malignity. 'She'll be forgotten as though she never existed, in a little while; and as for that Vaughan woman, she's several grades lower still, and ought only to be employed for the *London Journal*!'

Granton looked at him, and bit his lips to hide a smile.

'It strikes me you'd rather like to stand in Lady Carlyon's shoes, all the same, Mr. Grovelyn,' he said.

Grovelyn laughed, with such a shrill sound in the laughter, that Dr. Dalley immediately made a mental note entitled 'Splenetic Hysteria,' and watched him with professional eagerness.

'Not I,' he exclaimed. 'Everybody knows her husband writes more than half her books!'

'That's a lie!' said a full, clear voice behind them. 'Her husband is as big an ass as you are!'

Grovelyn turned round fiercely, and confronted Paul Valdis. There was a silence of surprise and consternation. Several men rose from various parts of the room, and came to see what was going on. Dr. Dalley rubbed his hands in delightful anticipation of a 'row,' but no one spoke or moved to interfere. The two men, Grovelyn and Valdis, stood face to face; the one mean-featured, with every movement of his body marked by a false and repulsive affectation, the other a manly and heroic figure distinguished by good looks and grace of bearing, with the consciousness of right and justice flashing in his eyes.

'You accuse me of telling a lie, Mr. Valdis,' hissed Grovelyn, 'and you call me an ass!'

'I do,' retorted Valdis, coolly. 'It is certainly a lie that Lord Carlyon writes half his wife's books. I had a letter from him once, and found out by it that he didn't known how to spell, much less express himself grammatically. And of course you are an ass if you think he could do anything in the way of literature; but you don't think so—you only say so out of pure jealousy of a woman's fame!'

'You shall answer for this, Mr. Valdis!' exclaimed Grovelyn, the curls of his door-mat coiffure bristling with rage. 'By Heaven, you shall answer for it!'

'When you please, and how you please,' returned Valdis, composedly; 'Now and here, if you like, and if the members permit fighting on the club premises.'

Exclamations of 'No, no!' mingled with laughter, partially drowned his voice. Everyone at the 'Bohemian' knew and dreaded Valdis; he was the most influential person on the committee, and the most dangerous if offended.

'Lady Carlyon's name is hardly fitted to be a bone of contention for us literary and play-acting dogs-in-the-manger,' he continued. 'She does not write verse, so she is not in your way, Mr. Grovelyn, nor will she interfere with your claim on posterity. She is not an actress, so she does not rob me of any of my honours as an actor, and I think we should do well to magnanimously allow her the peaceful enjoyment of her honestly-earned reputation, without grouping ourselves together like dirty street-boys to try and throw mud at her. Our mud doesn't stick, you know! Her book is an overwhelming success, and her husband will doubtless enjoy all the financial profits of it.'

He turned on his heel and looked over some papers lying on the table. Grovelyn touched his arm; there was an evil leer on his face.

'The pen is mightier than the sword, Mr. Valdis!' he observed.

'Ay, ay! That means you are going to blackguard me in the next number of the ha'penny *Clarion*? Be it so! Truth shall not budge for a ha'porth of slander!'

He resumed his perusal of the papers, and Grovelyn walked away slowly, his eyes fixed on the ground, and a brooding mischief in his face.

'You should never ruffle the temper of a man who has liver complaint, Valdis,' said Dr. Dalley, cheerfully, drawing his chair up to the table where the handsome actor still leaned. 'All evil humours come from the troubles of that important organ, and I am sure, if I could only meet a would-be murderer in time, I could save him from the committal of his intended wicked deed by a dose—quite a small dose—of suitable medicine!'

Valdis laughed rather forcedly.

'Could you? Then you'd better attend to Grovelyn without delay. He's ripe for murder—with the pen!'

Dr. Dalley rubbed his well-shaven, rounded chin meditatively.

'Is he? Well, perhaps he is; I really shouldn't wonder! Curiously enough, now I come to think of it, he has certain points about him that are synonymous with a murderer's instinct—phrenologically and physiologically speaking, I mean. It is rather strange he should be a poet at all.'

'Is he a poet?' queried Valdis, contemptuously; 'I never heard it honestly admitted. One does not acknowledge a man as a poet simply because he has a shock head of very dirty hair.'

'My dear Valdis,' expostulated the little doctor, amiably, 'you really are very bitter, almost violent in your strictures upon the man, who to me is one of the most interesting persons I have ever met! Because I foresee his death—due to very complex and entertaining complications of disease—in the space of—let me see! Well, suppose we say eighteen months! I do not think we shall have any chance of an autopsy. I wish I could think it likely, but I am afraid—' Here Dr. Dalley shook his head, and looked so despondent concerning the slender hope he had of dissecting Grovelyn after death, that Valdis laughed heartily, and this time unrestrainedly.

'You forget, there's the new photography; you could photograph his interior while he's alive!'

'By Jove! I never thought of that!' cried the doctor, joyfully; 'Of course! I'll have it done when the disease has made a little more progress. It will be extremely instructive!'

'It will,' said Valdis. 'Especially if you reproduce it in the journals, and call it "Portrait of a Lampooner's Interior under Process of Destruction by the Microbes of Disappointment and Envy."'

'Good! good!' chuckled Dalley, 'And, my dear Valdis, how would you like a photo entitled, "Portrait of a Distinguished Actor's Imaginative Organism consumed by the Fires of a Hopeless Love?"'

Valdis coloured violently, and anon grew pale.

'You are an old friend of mine, Dalley,' he said slowly, 'but you may go too far!'

MARIE CORELLI

'So I may, and so I have!' returned the little doctor, penitently, and with an abashed look. 'Forgive me, my dear boy; I've been guilty of a piece of impertinence, and I'm sorry! There! But I should like a few words with you alone, if you don't mind. It's Sunday night; you can't go and be "Ernani." Will you waste a few minutes of your company on me—outside these premises, where the very walls have ears?'

Valdis assented, and in a few minutes they left the club together. With their departure there was a slight stir among the men in the room, who were reading, smoking, and drinking whisky and water.

'I wish she'd take up with him!' growled one man, whose head was half hidden behind a *Referee*. 'Why the devil doesn't she play the fool like other women?'

'Whom are you speaking of?' inquired a stout personage, who was busy correcting his critical notes on a new play which had been acted for the first time the previous evening.

'Delicia Vaughan—Lady Carlyon,' answered the first man. 'Valdis is infatuated with her. Why she doesn't go over to him, I can't imagine; a writing female need not be more particular than a dancing female, I should say they're both public characters, and Carlyon has thrown himself down as a free gift at the feet of La Marina, so there's no obstacle in the way, except the woman's own extraordinary "cussedness."'

'What good would it do you that she should "go over," as you call it, to Valdis?' inquired the stout scribbler, dubiously, biting the end of his pencil.

'Good? Why, none to me in particular,' said the other, 'but it would drag her down! Don't you see? It would prove to the idiotic public, that is just now running after her as if she were a goddess, that she is only the usual frail stuff of which women are made. I should like that! I confess I should like it! I like women to keep in their places—'

'That is, on the down grade,' suggested the stout gentleman, still dubiously.

'Of course! what else were they made for? La Marina, who kicks up her skirts, and hits her nose with the point of her big toe, is far more of a woman, I take it, and certainly more to the taste of a man, than the insolent, brilliant, superior Delicia Vaughan!'

'Oh! You admit she is brilliant and superior?' said the stout critic, with a smile. 'Well, you know that's saying a great deal! I'm an old-fashioned man—'

'Of course you are!' put in a young fellow, standing near. 'You like to believe there may be good women,—real angels,—on earth; you like to believe it, and so do I!'

He was a fresh-coloured youth, lately come up to London from the provinces to try his hand at literature; and the individual with the *Referee*, who had started the conversation, glanced him over with the supremest contempt.

'I hope your mother's in town to take care of you, you ninny,' he said. 'You're a very callow bird!'

The young man laughed good-naturedly.

'Am I? Well, all the same, I'd rather honour women than despise them.'

The stout critic looked up from his notebook approvingly.

'Keep that up as long as you can, youngster,' he said. 'It won't hurt you!'

A silence followed; the man with the *Referee* spoke not another word, and the fresh-coloured provincial, getting tired of the smoke and the general air of egotistical self-concentration with which each member of the club sat fast in his own chosen chair, absorbed in his own chosen form of inward meditation, took a hasty departure, glad to get out into the cool night air. His way home lay through a part of Mayfair, and at one of the houses he passed he saw a long line of carriages outside and a brilliant display of light within. Some fashionable leader of society was holding a Sunday evening reception; and moved by a certain vague interest and curiosity, the young reporter lingered for a moment watching the gaily-dressed women passing in and out. While he yet waited, a dignified butler appeared on the steps and murmured something in the ear of a gold-buttoned commissionaire, who thereupon shouted vociferously,—

'Lady Car-ly-on's carriage! This way!'

And as an elegant *coupé*, drawn by two spirited horses drove swiftly up in response to the summons, a woman wrapped in a soft, white mantilla of old Spanish lace, and holding up her silken train with one hand, came out of the house with a gentleman, evidently her host, who was escorting her to the carriage. The young man from the country leaned eagerly forward and caught sight of a proud, delicate face illumined by two dark violet eyes, a flashing glimpse of beauty that vanished ere fully seen. But it was enough to make him who had been called a 'callow bird' wax suddenly indignant with certain self-styled celebrities he had just left behind at the 'Bohemian.'

'What beasts they are!' he muttered; 'what cads! Thank God they'll never be famous; they're too mean! To fling their dirty spite at a woman like that! It's disgusting! Wait till I get a chance; I'll "review" their trash for them!'

And warmed by the prospect of this future vengeance, the 'callow bird' went home to roost.

IV

Some days after the war of words between Valdis and Aubrey Grovelyn at the 'Bohemian,' Delicia was out shopping in Bond Street, not for herself, but for her husband. She had a whole list of orders to execute for him, from cravats and hosiery up to a new and expensive 'coach-luncheon-basket,' to which he had taken a sudden fancy; and besides this, she was looking about in all the jeweller's shops for some tasteful and valuable thing to give him as a souvenir of the approaching anniversary of their marriage day. Pausing at last in front of one glittering window, she saw a rather quaint set of cuff-studs which she thought might possibly answer her purpose, and she went inside the shop to examine them more closely. The jeweller, not knowing her personally, but judging from the indifferent way in which she took the announcement of his rather stiff prices, that she must be a tolerably rich woman, began to show her some of his most costly pieces of workmanship, hoping thereby to tempt her into the purchase of something for herself. She had no very great love for jewels, but she had for artistic design, and she gratified the jeweller by her intelligent praise of some particularly choice bits, the merits of which could only be fully recognised by a quick eye and cultivated taste.

'That is a charming pendant,' she said, taking up a velvet case, in which rested a dove with outspread wings, made of the finest diamonds, carrying in its beak the facsimile of a folded letter in finely-wrought gold, with the words, *'Je t'adore ma mie!'* set upon it in lustrous rubies. 'The idea is graceful in itself, and admirably carried out.'

The jeweller smiled.

'Ah, that's a very unique thing,' he said, 'but it's not for sale. It has been made to special order for Lord Carlyon.'

A faint tremor passed over Delicia like the touch of a cold wind, and for a moment the jewels spread out on the glass counter before her danced up and down like sparks flying out of a fire, but she maintained her outward composure. And in another minute she smiled at herself, wondering why she had been so startled, for, of course, her husband had ordered this pretty piece of jewellery as a gift for her, on the very anniversary she was preparing to celebrate by a gift to him! Meanwhile the jeweller, who was of an open mind, and rather fond of confiding bits of gossip to stray customers, took the diamond dove out of its

MARIE CORELLI

satin-lined nest, and held it up in the sunlight to show the lustre of the stones.

'It's a lovely design!' he said enthusiastic-ally; 'It will cost Lord Carlyon a little over five hundred pounds. But gentlemen of his sort never mind what they pay, so long as they can please the lady they are after. And the lady in this case isn't his lordship's wife, as you may well suppose!'

He sniggered, and one of his eyelids trembled as though it were on the point of a profane wink. Delicia regarded him with a straight, clear look.

'Why should I suppose anything of the sort?' she queried calmly. 'I should, on the contrary, imagine that it was just the tasteful gift a man would wish to choose for his wife.'

The jeweller made a curious little bow over his counter, implying deference towards Delicia's unsuspicious nature.

'Would you really?' he said. 'Well, now, as a matter of fact, in our trade, when we get special orders from gentlemen for valuable jewels, they are never by any chance intended for the gentlemen's wives. Of course it is not our business to interfere with, or even comment upon the actions of our customers; but as far as our own artistic work goes, it often pains us—yes, I may say it pains us—to see some of our finest pieces being thrown away on dancers and music-hall singers, who don't really know how to appreciate them, because they haven't the taste or culture for it. They know the money's worth of jewels—oh, you may trust them for that. And whenever they want to raise cash, why, of course their jewels come handy. But it's not satisfactory to us as a firm, for we take a good deal of pride in our work. This dove, for instance,' and again he dangled the pendant in the sunbeams, 'It's a magnificent specimen of diamond-setting, and of course we, as the producers of such a piece, would far rather know it was going to Lady Carlyon than to La Marina.'

Delicia began to feel as if she were in a kind of dull dream; there were flickering lines of light flashing before her eyes, and her limbs trembled. She heard the jeweller's voice, going on again in its politely gossiping monotone, as though it were a long way off.

'Of course La Marina is a wonderful creature, a marvellous dancer, and good-looking in her way, but common. Ah! common's no word for it! She was the daughter of a costermonger in Eastcheap. Now, Lady Carlyon is a very different person; she is best known by her maiden name, Delicia Vaughan. She's the author of that name; I daresay you may have read some of her books?'

'I believe—yes, I think I have,' murmured Delicia, faintly.

'Well, there you are! She's a really famous woman, and very much loved by many people, I've heard say; but, lord! her husband hardly gives her a thought! I've seen him in this very street walking with females that even I'd be ashamed to know; and it's rumoured that he hasn't got a penny of his own, and that all the money he throws about so lavishly is his wife's; and if that's the case, it's really shameful, because of course she, without knowing it, pays for Marina's jewels! However, there's no accounting for tastes. I suppose Lady Carlyon's too clever, or else plain in her personal appearance; and that's why this diamond dove is going to La Marina instead of to her. Will you take the cuff-studs?'

'Yes, thank you, I will take them,' said Delicia, opening her purse with cold, trembling fingers, and counting out crisp bank-notes to the value of twenty pounds. 'They are pretty, and very suitable for a—a gentleman.'

Unconsciously she laid an emphasis on the word 'gentleman,' and the jeweller nodded.

'Exactly! There's nothing vulgar about them, not the least suspicion of anything 'fast'! Really you can't be too particular in the choice of studs, for what with the sporting men, and the jockeys and trainers who get presents of valuable studs from their turf patrons, it's difficult to hit upon anything really gentlemanly *for* a gentleman. But'—and the worthy man smiled as he packed up the studs—'after all, real gentleman are getting very scarce! Allow me!' Here he flung open the door of his establishment with the grace of a Sir Charles Grandison, and royally issued his command to the small boy in buttons attached to the shop, 'See this lady to her carriage!'

How 'this lady' got into that carriage she never quite knew. The page boy did his part in carefully attending to her dress that it should not touch the wheel, in wrapping her round with the rich bear-skin rug that protected her from side winds, and in quietly grasping the shilling she slipped into his palm for his services, but she herself felt more like a mechanical doll moving on wires than a living, feeling woman. Her coachman, who always had enough to do in the management of the spirited horses which drew her light victoria, glanced back at her once or twice doubtfully, as he guided his prancing animals out of the confusion of Bond Street and drove towards the Park, considering within himself

MARIE CORELLI

that, if he were going in an undesired direction, 'her ladyship' would speedily stop him; but her ladyship lay back in her cushioned seat, inert, indifferent, seeing nothing and hearing nothing. The fashionable pageant of the Park 'season' seemed to her a mere chaotic whirl; and several eager admirers of her beauty and her genius raised their hats to her in vain—she never perceived them. A curious numbness had crept over her; she wondered, as she felt the movement of the carriage, whether it was not a hearse, and she the dead body within it being carried to her grave! Then, quite suddenly, she raised herself and sat upright, glancing about at the rich foliage of the trees, the gay flower-beds and the up-and-down moving throng of people; a bright flush reddened her face, which for the past few minutes had been deadly pale, and as two or three of her acquaintances passed her in their carriages or on foot, she saluted them with her usual graceful air of mingled pride and sweetness, and seemed almost herself again. But she was not long able to endure the strain she put upon her nerves, and after one or two turns in the Row, she bade her coachman drive home. Arrived there, she found a telegram from her husband, running thus:—

'Shall not return to dinner. Don't wait up for me.'

Crushing the missive in her hand, she went to her own study immediately, the faithful Spartan following her, and there she shut herself up alone with her dog friend for a couple of hours. The scholarly peace of the place had its effect in soothing her, and in allaying the burning smart of her wounded spirit; and with a sigh of relief she sat down in her favourite arm-chair with her back purposely turned to the white marble 'Antinous,' whose cruel smile had nothing but mockery in it for a woman's pain. Spartan laid his head on her knee, and she rested one hand caressingly on his broad brow.

'I must think this worry out, Spartan!' she said gently. 'I feel as if I had swallowed poison and needed an antidote.'

Spartan wagged his bushy tail and looked volumes. Had he been able to speak, he might have said, 'Why did you ever trust a man? Dogs are much more faithful!'

She sank into a profound reverie. Her brain was clear, logical and evenly balanced, and she had none of the flighty, fantastical, hysterical notions common to many of her sex. She had been trained, or rather, she had trained herself, in the splendid school of classic philosophy;

and in addition to this, she was a devout Christian, one of the old-world type, who would have willingly endured martyrdom for the faith had it been necessary. She was not a church-goer, and she belonged to no special 'sect;' she had no vulgar vices to hide by an ostentatious display of public charities, but she had the most absolute and passionate belief in, and love for Christ, as the one Divine Messenger from God to man; and now she was bringing both her faith and her philosophic theories to bear on the present unexpected crisis in her life.

'If I were a low woman, a vulgar woman, a virago in domestic life, or what the French call *une femme impossible*, I could understand his seeking a change from my detestable company anywhere and everywhere,' she mentally argued; 'but as things are, what have I done that he should descend from me to La Marina? Men will amuse themselves—I know that well enough—but need the amusement be obtained on such a low grade! And is it fair that my earnings should keep La Marina in jewels?'

At this latter thought she started up and began to pace the room restlessly. In so doing she came face to face with the marble bust of 'Antinous,' and she stopped abruptly, looking full at it.

'Oh men, what were you made for?' she demanded, half aloud. 'To be masters of the planet? Then surely your mastership should be characterised by truth and nobility, not vileness and fraud! Surely God originally intended you for better things than to trample under your feet all the weak and helpless, to work ravage on the fairest scenes in nature, and to make miserable wrecks of all the women that love you! Yes, Antinous, I can read in your sculptured face the supreme Egotism of manhood, an Egotism which fate will avenge in its own good time! No wonder so few men are real Christians; it is too sublime and spiritual a creed for the male nature, which is a composition of wild beast and intellectual pagan. Now, what shall be my course of action? Shall I, Delicia, seeing my husband in the mud, go down into the mud also? Or shall I keep clean—not only clean in body but clean in mind? Clean from meanness, clean from falsehood, clean from spite, not only for his sake, but for the sake of my own self-respect? Shall I let things take their course until they culminate of themselves in the pre-ordained catastrophe that always follows evil? Yes, I think I will! Life after all is a shadow; and love, what is it?' She sighed and shuddered. 'Less than a shadow, perchance; but there is something in me which must outlast both life and love—something which is the real Delicia, who must hereafter answer to a Supreme Judge for the thoughts which have elevated or degraded her soul!'

She resumed her pacing to and fro.

'How easy it would be to act like other women!' she mused; 'to rant and weep, and hysterically shriek complaints in the ears of "my lord" when he returns to-night; or begin the day to-morrow with fume and fuss as hot and steaming as the boiling water with which I make the breakfast tea! Or to go and grumble to a female *confidante* who would at once sell her information for five shillings to the most convenient "society journal!" Or to sink right down into the deepest mire of infamy and write anonymous letters to La Marina, daughter of the green-grocer in Eastcheap! Or employ a detective to dodge his movements and hers! Heavens! How low we can fall if we choose! and equally how high we can stand if we determine to take a firm footing on

> *"Some snow-crowned peak,*
> *Lofty and glittering in the golden glow*
> *Of summer's ripening splendour."*

Some people ask what is the good of "standing high?" Certainly you get on much better, in society at least, if you creep low, and crawl on very humble all-fours to the feet of the latest *demi-mondaine*, provided she be of the aristocracy. If you know how to condone the vulgarity of a prince and call his vices virtue, if you can pardon the blackguardism of a duke and speak of him as a "gentleman," in spite of the fact that he is not fit to be tolerated among decent-minded people, you are sure to "get on," as the phrase goes. To keep oneself morally clean is a kind of offence nowadays; but methinks I shall continue to offend!' She passed her hand across her forehead dreamily. 'Something has confused and stunned me; I cannot quite realise what it is. I think I had an idol somewhere, set up on a pedestal of gold; it has suddenly tumbled down of its own accord!' She smiled vaguely. 'It is not broken yet, but it has certainly fallen!'

That night, when Lord Carlyon returned about one o'clock, he found the house dark and silent. No one was waiting up for him but his valet, a discreet and sober individual who knew his master's secrets and kept them; not at all because he respected his master, but because he respected his master's wife. And the semi-obscurity and grave solitude of his home irritated 'Beauty' Carlyon to a most inconsistent degree, inasmuch as he had himself telegraphed to Delicia that she was not to sit up for him.

'Where is her ladyship?' he demanded haughtily. 'Did she go out this evening?'

Gravely the valet assisted him to pull off his opera coat as he replied,—

'No, sir—my lord, I mean—her ladyship dined alone, and retired early. I believe the maid said her ladyship was in bed by ten.'

Carlyon grumbled something inaudible and went upstairs. Outside his wife's room he paused and tried the handle of her bedroom door; it was locked. Surprised and angry, he rapped smartly on the panels; there was no answer save a low, fierce growl from Spartan, who, suddenly rising from his usual post on the landing outside his mistress's sleeping chamber, manifested unusual and extraordinary signs of temper.

'Down, you fool!' muttered Carlyon, addressing the huge beast. 'Lie down, or it will be the worse for you!'

But Spartan remained erect, with ears flattened and white teeth a-snarl, and Carlyon, after rapping once more vainly at the closed door, gave it up as a bad job and retired to his own private room.

'Never knew her so dead asleep before,' he grumbled. 'She generally stays awake till I come home.'

He flung himself into his bed with a kind of sullen rage upon him; things had gone altogether very wrong with him that evening. He had lost money (Delicia's money) at play, and La Marina had been in what her intimates called 'one of her nasty humours.' That is, she had drunk a great deal more champagne than was good for her, and had afterwards exhibited a tendency to throw wine glasses at her admirers. She had boxed Carlyon's ears, put a spoonful of strawberry ice down his back, and called him 'a ha'porth of bad aristocrat.'

'What do you suppose we *artistes* marry such fellows as you for?' she had yelled, with a burst of tipsy laughter. 'Why, to make you look greater fools than ever!'

And then she had shot a burnt almond nearly into his eye. And he had endured all this stoically, for the mere stupid satisfaction of having the other men round La Marina's supper-table understand that she was his property at present, no matter to whom she might hereafter belong. But she had behaved so badly, and she had treated him with such ingratitude, that he, unconsciously to himself, longed for the fair, calm presence of Delicia, who always received him with the honour and worship he considered due to him as a man, a lord, and an officer in the Guards; and now when he came home, expecting to be charmed and flattered and caressed by her, she had committed the unwarrantable indiscretion of going to bed and falling sound asleep! It was really too bad!—enough to sting the lofty spirit of a Carlyon! And such is the curious self-pity and egotism of some men at their worst, that 'his lordship' felt himself to be a positively injured man as he settled his 'god-like' head upon his lonely pillow, and fell into an uneasy slumber, disturbed by very unpleasant dreams of his losses at baccarat, and the tipsy rages of Marina.

V

Next morning Delicia rose at about six o'clock and went out riding in the Row long before the fashionable world was astir. Attended by her groom and Spartan, who took long racing gambols on the grass beyond the railings of the 'Ladies' Mile,' she cantered under the deep, dewy shade of the trees, and thought out her position in regard to her husband. In spite of inward grief and perplexity, she had slept well; for to a clear conscience and pure heart, combined with a healthy state of body, sleep is never denied. Mother Nature specially protects her straightforward and cleanly children; she keeps their faces young, their eyes bright, their spirits elastic, their tempers equable, and for the soothing of Delicia's trouble this morning, the sunbeams danced about her in a golden waltz of pleasure, the leaves rustled in the wind, the flowers exhaled their purest fragrance and the birds sang. Riding easily on her beautiful mare 'Phillida'—who was almost as much a personal friend of hers as Spartan himself, and whom she had purchased out of the 'royalties' accumulating on one of her earlier works—she found herself more than usually receptive of the exquisite impressions of natural loveliness. She was aware of everything; from the white clouds that were heaped in snowy, mountainous ranges along the furthest visible edge of the blue sky, to the open-hearted daisies in the grass that stared up at the lately-risen sun with all the frankness of old friendship and familiarity. The fresh morning air and the exhilarating exercise sent a lovely colour to her cheeks, and as her graceful form swayed lightly to the half-coquettish, gay cantering of 'Phillida,' who was also conscious that it was a very agreeable morning, she felt as if the information she had so unexpectedly and reluctantly received in the jeweller's shop in Bond Street on the previous day was a bad dream and nothing more. After about an hour's riding she returned home at a quick trot, and on entering the house heard that her 'lord and master' had not yet risen. She changed her riding habit for one of her simple white morning gowns, and went into her study to open and read her numerous letters, and mark them in order for her secretary to answer. She was still engaged in this occupation when Lord Carlyon came down, slowly, sleepily, and in no very good humour.

'Oh, there you are at last, Will!' she said, looking up at him brightly. 'You came home late last night, I suppose, and are tired?'

He stood still for a moment, wondering within himself why she did not give him her usual good-morning kiss.

'It was not so very late,' he said crossly. 'It was only half-past twelve. You've often stayed awake waiting for me later than that. But last night, when I knocked at your door, you never answered me—you must have been dead asleep.'

This in a tone of injury.

Delicia read calmly through the letter she held in her hand, then set it aside.

'Yes, I must have been,' she replied tranquilly. 'You see I work pretty hard, and nature is good enough to give me rest when I need it. You work hard too, Will, but in quite another way—you toil after amusement. Now that's the hardest form of labour I know! Treadmills are nothing to it! No wonder you're tired! Breakfast's ready; let us go and have it; I've been out riding for an hour this morning, and I feel desperately hungry. Come along!'

She led the way downstairs; he followed slowly and with a vague feeling of uneasiness. He missed something in his wife's manner—an indefinable something which he could not express—something that had always characterised her, but which now had unaccountably disappeared. It was as if a wide river had suddenly rolled in between them, forcing her to stand on one side of the flood and he on the other. He studied her observantly from under his fine eyelash growth, as she made the tea and with a few quick touches here and there altered the decorous formality of the breakfast-table into the similitude of an Arcadian feast of beauty by the mere artistic placing of a vase of flowers or a dish of fruit, and this done, handed him the morning's newspaper with smiling and courteous punctilio.

'Spartan seems to be turning crusty,' he remarked as he unfolded the journal. 'Last night, when I knocked at your door, he showed his teeth and growled at me. I didn't know he had such an uncertain temper.'

Delicia looked round at her canine friend with a pretty air of remonstrance.

'Oh, Spartan! What is this I hear?' she said, whereat Spartan hung his head and tucked his tail well under his haunches. 'Don't you know your master when he comes home late? Did you take him for a regular "rake," Spartan? Did you think he had been in bad company? Fie, for shame! You ought to know better, naughty boy!'

Spartan looked abashed, but not so abashed as did Lord Carlyon. He fidgeted on his chair, got red in the face, and made a great noise in folding and unfolding the newspaper; and presently, finding his own thoughts too much for him, he began to get angry with nobody in particular, and, as is the fashion with egotistical men, turned a sudden unprovoked battery of assault on the woman he was hourly and daily wronging.

'I heard something last night that displeased me very much, Delicia,' he said, affecting a high moral tone. 'It concerns you, and I should like to speak to you about it.'

'Yes?' said Delicia, with the very slightest lifting of her delicate eyebrows.

'Yes.' And Lord Carlyon hummed and hawed for a couple of dubious seconds. 'You see, you are a woman, and you ought to be very careful what you write. A man told me that in your last book there were some very strong passages,—really strong—you know what I mean—and he said that it is very questionable whether any woman with a proper sense of delicacy ought to write in such a manner.'

Delicia looked at him steadily.

'Who is he? My book has probably touched him on a sore place!'

Carlyon did not answer immediately; he was troubled with an awkward cough.

'Well,' he said at last, 'it was Fitz-Hugh; you know him—an awfully good fellow,—has sisters and all that—says he wouldn't let his sisters read your book for the world, and it was deuced disagreeable for me to hear, I can tell you.'

'You have read my book,' said Delicia, slowly; 'and did you discover anything of the nature complained of by Captain Fitz-Hugh?'

Again Lord Carlyon coughed uncomfortably.

'Well, upon my word, I don't exactly remember now, but I can't say I did!'

Delicia still kept her eyes fixed upon him.

'Then, of course, you defended me?'

Carlyon flushed, and began to butter a piece of toast in nervous haste.

'Why, there was no need for defence,' he stammered. 'The whole thing is in a nutshell—an author's an author, man or woman, and there's an end of it. Of course you're alone responsible for the book, and, as I said, if he don't like it he needn't read it, and no one asked him to give it to his sisters!'

'You prevaricate,' interrupted Delicia, steadily; 'But perhaps it is as well you did not think it necessary to defend me to such a man as Captain Fitz-Hugh, who for years has been the notorious lover of Lady Rapley, to the disgrace of her husband who permits the scandal. And for Captain Fitz-Hugh's sisters, who are the chief purveyors of slander in the wretched little provincial town where they live, each one of them trying her best to catch the curate or the squire, I shall very willingly write a book some day that deals solely with the petty lives lived by such women—women more unclean in mind than a Swift, and lower in the grade of intellect than an aspiring tadpole, who at any rate has the laudable ambition and intention of becoming an actual frog some day!'

Carlyon stared, vaguely startled and chilled by her cold, calm accents.

'By Jove! You *are* cutting, you know, Delicia!' he expostulated. 'Poor Fitz-Hugh! he can't help himself falling in love with Lady Rapley—'

'Can't help himself!' echoed Delicia, with supreme scorn. 'Can he not help disgracing her? Is it not Possible to love greatly and nobly, and die with the secret kept? Is there no dignity left in manhood? Or in womanhood? Do you think, for instance, that *I* would permit myself to love any other man but you?'

His handsome face flushed, and his eyes kindled. He smiled a self-satisfied smile.

'Upon my life, that's splendid—the way you say that!' he exclaimed. 'But all women are not like you—'

'I know they are not,' she replied. 'Captain Fitz-Hugh's sisters, for example, are certainly not at all like me! They do well to avoid my book; they would find female cant and hypocrisy too openly exposed there to please them. But with regard to your complaint—for I regard it to be a complaint from you—you may challenge the whole world of slander-mongers, if you like, to point to one offensive expression in my writings—they will never find it.'

He rose and put his arm round her. At his touch she shuddered with a new and singular aversion. He thought the tremor one of delight.

'And so you will never permit yourself to love any other man but me?' he asked caressingly, touching the rich masses of her hair with his lips.

'Never!' she responded firmly, looking straight into his eyes. 'But do not misunderstand my meaning! It is very possible that I might cease to love you altogether—yes, it certainly might happen at any moment; but I should never, because of this, love another man. I could not so degrade myself as to parcel my affections out in various quarters, after the fashion of Lady Rapley, who has descended voluntarily, as one of our latter-day novelists observes, "to the manners and customs of the poultry yard." If I ceased to love you, then love itself for me would cease. It could never revive for anyone else; it would be dead dust and ashes! I have no faith in women who love more than once.'

Carlyon still toyed with her hair; the undefinable something he missed in her fretted and perplexed him.

'Are you aware that you look at me very strangely this morning, Delicia?' he said at last; 'Almost as if I were not the same man! And this is the first time I have ever heard you speak of the possibility of your ceasing to love me!'

She moved restlessly in his embrace, and presently, gently putting him aside, rose from the breakfast-table and pretended to busy herself with the arrangement of some flowers on the mantelpiece.

'I have been reading philosophy,' she answered him, with a tremulous little laugh. 'Grim old cynics, both ancient and modern, who say that nothing lasts on earth, and that the human soul is made of such imperishable stuff that it is always out-reaching one emotion after another and striving to attain the highest perfection. If this be true, then even human love is poor and trifling compared to love divine!' Her eyes darkened with intensity of feeling. 'At least, so say some of our sage instructors; and if it be indeed a fact that mortal things are but the passing shadow of immortal ones, it is natural enough that we should gradually outlive the temporal in our desire for the eternal.'

Carlyon looked at her wonderingly; she met his gaze fully, her eyes shining with a pure light that almost dazzled him.

'I can't follow all your transcendental theories,' he said, half pettishly; 'I never could. I have always told you that you can't get reasoning men to care about any other life than this one—they don't see it; they don't want it. Heaven doesn't suggest itself to them as at all a jolly sort of place, and you know, if you come to think of it, you'd rather not have an angel to love you; you'd much rather have a woman.'

'Speak for yourself, my dear Will,' answered Delicia, with a slight smile. 'If angels, such as I imagine them to be, exist at all, I should much prefer to be loved by one of them than by a man. The angel's love might last; the man's would not. We see these things from different points of view. And as for this life, I assure you I am not at all charmed with it.'

'Good heavens! You've got everything you want,' exclaimed Carlyon, 'Even fame, which so rarely attends a woman!'

'Yes, and I know the value of it!' she responded. 'Fame, literally translated, means slander. Do you think I am not able to estimate it at its true worth? Do you think I am ignorant of the fact that I am followed by the lies and envies and hatreds of the unsuccessful? Or that I shut my eyes to the knowledge of the enmity that everywhere pursues me? If I were old, if I were poor, if I were ugly, and had scarcely a gown to my back, and still wrote books, I should be much more liked than I am. I daresay some rich people might even be found willing to "patronise" me!' She laughed disdainfully. 'But when these same rich people discover that I can afford to patronise *them*,—who is there that can rightly estimate the measure or the violence of their antipathy for me? Yet when I say I am not charmed with life, I only mean the "social" life; I do not mean the life of nature—of that I am never tired.'

'Well, this morning, at any rate, you appear to be tired of me,' said Carlyon, irritably. 'So I suppose I'd better get out of your way!'

She made no answer whatever. He fidgeted about a little, then began to grumble again.

'I'm sorry you're in such a bad humour.' At this she raised her eyebrows in smiling protest. 'Yes, you know you're in a bad humour,' he went on obstinately; 'you pretend you're not, but you are. And I wanted to ask you a question on your own business affairs.'

'Pray ask it!' said Delicia, still smiling. 'Though, before you speak, let me assure you my business affairs are in perfect order.'

'Oh, I don't know,' he went on uneasily; 'these d——d publishers often wriggle out of bargains, and try to "do" a woman. That firm, now—the one that has just published your last book—have they paid you?'

'They have,' she answered with composure. 'They are, though publishers, still honourable men.'

'It was to be eight thousand, wasn't it?' he asked, looking down at the lapels of his well-fitting morning-coat and flicking a speck of dust off the cloth.

'It was, and it is,' she answered. 'I paid four thousand of it into your bank yesterday.'

His eyes flashed.

'By Jove! What a clever little woman you are!' he exclaimed. 'Fancy getting all that cash out of your brain-pan! It's quite a mystery to me how you do it, you know! I can never make it out—'

'There's no accounting for the public taste,' said Delicia, watching him with the pained consciousness of a sudden contempt. 'But you need not puzzle yourself over the matter.'

'Oh, I never bother my head over literature at all!' laughed Carlyon, becoming quite hilarious, now that he knew an extra four thousand pounds had been piled into his private banking account. 'People often ask me, "How does your wife manage to write such clever books?" And I always reply, "Don't know, never could tell. Astonishing woman! Shuts herself up in her own room like a silkworm, and spins a regular cocoon!" That's what I say, you know; yet nobody ever seems to believe me, and lots of fellows swear you *must* get a man to help you.'

'It is part of man's conceit to imagine his assistance always necessary,' said Delicia, coldly smiling. 'Considering how loudly men talk of their own extraordinary abilities, it is really astonishing how little they manage to do. Good-bye! I'm going upstairs to spin cocoons.'

He stopped her as she moved to leave the room.

'I say, Delicia, it's awfully sweet of you to hand over that four thousand—'

She gave a little gesture of offence.

'Why speak of it, Will? You know that half of every sum I earn is placed to your account; it has been my rule ever since our marriage, and there is really no need to allude to what is now a mere custom of business.'

He still held her arm.

'Yes, that's all very well; but look here, Delicia, you're not angry with me for anything, are you?'

She raised her head and looked straightly at him.

'No, Will—not angry.'

Something in her eyes intimidated him. He checked himself abruptly, afraid to ask her anything more.

'Oh, that's all right,' he stammered hurriedly. 'I'm glad you're not angry. I thought you seemed a little put out; but it's jolly that I'm mistaken, you know. Ta-ta! Have a good morning's grind.'

'And as she went, he drew out a cigar from his silver case with rather shaking fingers, and pretended to be absorbed in lighting it. When it was finally lit and he looked up, she was gone. With a sigh, he flung himself into an arm-chair and puffed away at his choice Havana in a sore and miserable confusion of mind. No human being, perhaps, is quite so sore and miserable as a man who is born with the instincts of a gentleman

MARIE CORELLI

and yet conducts himself like a cad. There are many such tramps of a decayed and dying gentility amongst us—men with vague glimmerings of the ancient chivalry of their race lying dormant within them, who yet lack the force of will necessary to plan their lives resolutely out upon those old-fashioned but grand foundations known as truth and loyalty. Because it is 'the thing' to talk slang, they pollute the noble English language with coarse expressions copied from stable conversation; and because it is considered 'swagger' to make love to other men's wives, they enter into this base form of vulgar intrigue almost as if it were a necessary point of dignity and an added grace to manhood. If we admit that men are the superior and stronger sex, what a pitiable thing it is to note how little their moral forces assist in the elevation of woman, their tendency being to drag her down as low as possible! If she be unwedded, man does his best to compromise her; if he has married her, he frequently neglects her; if she be another's wife, he frequently tries to injure her reputation. This is 'modern' morality, exhibited to us in countless varying phases every day, detailed every morning and evening in our newspapers, witnessed over and over again through every 'season's' festivities; and this, combined with atheism, and an utter indifference as to the results of evil, is making of 'upper class' England a something worse than pagan Rome was just before its fall. The safety of the country is with what we elect to call the 'lower classes,' who are educating themselves slowly but none the less surely; but who, it must be remembered, are not yet free from savagery,—the splendid brute savagery which breaks out in all great nations when aristocratic uncleanness and avarice have gone too far,—a savagery which threw itself panting and furious upon the treacherous Marie Antoinette of France, with her beauty, her wicked wantonness, her thoughtless extravagance and luxury, and her cruel contempt for the poor, and never loosened its fangs till it had dragged her haughty head to the level of the scaffold, there to receive the just punishment of selfishness and pride. For punishment must fall sooner or later on every wilful misuser of life's opportunities; though had anyone told Lord Carlyon this by way of warning, he would have bidden him, in the choicest of 'swagger' terms, to 'go and be a rotten preacher!' And in saying so, he would have considered himself witty. Yet he knew well enough that his 'little affair' with La Marina was nothing but a deliberate dishonour done to his blameless wife; and he was careful to avoid thinking as to where the money came from as he flung it about at cards, or in restaurants, or on race-courses.

'After all,' he considered now, as he smoked his cigar leisurely, and allowed his mind to dwell comfortably on the reflection of that four thousand pounds placed to his account, 'she likes her work; she couldn't get on without it, and there's nothing so much in her handing me over half the "dibs" as she's got all the fame.'

And through some curious process of man's logic he managed to argue himself into a perfect state of satisfaction with the comfortable way the world was arranged for him through his wife's unremitting toil.

'Poor little soul!' he murmured placidly, glancing at his handsome face in an opposite mirror, 'She loves me awfully! This morning she half pretends she doesn't, but she would give every drop of blood in her body to save me from a pin-prick of trouble. And why shouldn't she? Women must have something to love; she's perfectly happy in her way, and so am I in mine.'

With which consoling conclusion he ended his meditations, and went out for the day as usual.

On returning home to dinner, however, he was considerably put out to find a note waiting for him in the hall; a note from his wife, running thus:—

'Shall not return to dinner. Am going to the "Empire" with the Cavendishes; do not wait up for me.'

'Well, I call that pretty cool!' he muttered angrily. 'Upon my word, I call that infernally cool!'

He marched about the hall, fuming and fretting for a minute or two, then he called his valet.

'Robson, I sha'n't want dinner served,' he said snappishly; 'I'm going out.'

'Very good, my lord.'

'Did her ladyship leave any message?'

'None, my lord. She merely said she was going to dine with Mr. and Mrs. Cavendish, and would probably not be back till late.'

He frowned like a spoilt child.

'Well, I sha'n't be back till late either, if at all,' he said fretfully. 'Just come and get me into my dress suit, will you?'

Robson followed him upstairs obediently, and bore with his caprices, which were many, during the business of attiring him for the evening. He was in an exceedingly bad humour, and gave vent to what the children call a 'bad swear' more than once. Finally he got into a hansom and was driven off at a rattling pace, the respectable Robson watching his departure from the open hall door.

'You're a nice one!' remarked that worthy personage, as the vehicle containing his master turned a sharp corner and disappeared. 'Up to no end of pranks; as bad and worse than if you was the regular son of a king! Yes, taking you on and off, one would almost give you credit for being a real prince, you've got so little conscience! But my lady's one too many for you, I fancy; she's quiet but she's clever; and I don't believe she'll keep her eyes shut much longer. She can't, if you're a-going on continual in the way you are.'

Thus Robson soliloquised, shutting the street door with a bang to emphasise the close of his half-audible observations. Then he went up into Delicia's study to give Spartan some dinner. Spartan received the plateful brought to him with majestic indifference, and an air which implied that he would attend to it presently. He had a little white glove of Delicia's between his paws, and manifested no immediate desire to disturb himself. He had his own canine ideas of love and fidelity; and though he was only a dog, it may be he had a higher conception of honour and truth than is attained by men, who, in the excess of self-indulgence, take all the benefits of love and good fortune as their 'rights,' and are destitute of even the saving grace of gratitude.

VI

It was no impetus of feminine recrimination or spite that had caused Delicia to go out on that particular evening, and thus deprive her husband of her society in the same abrupt fashion with which he had so often deprived her of his. Mr. and Mrs. Cavendish were old friends of hers. They had known her when she was a little orphan girl with no brothers or sisters—no companions of her own age to amuse her—nothing, in fact, but her own pensive and romantic thoughts, which had, though she then knew it not, helped to weave her now brilliant destiny. They were elderly, childless people, and they had always been devoted to Delicia, so that when Mrs. Cavendish paid an unexpected call in the afternoon and stated that she and her husband were 'mopy,' and that they would take it very kindly if Delicia would come and dine with them, and afterwards accompany them to the 'Empire,' for which they had a box near the stage, Delicia readily accepted the proposition as a welcome change from her own uncomfortable and unprofitable thoughts. To begin with, she had grown so accustomed now to her husband's telegrams announcing that he would not be back to dinner, that she accepted his absence as a far greater probability than his home-returning. Therefore she was glad of the chance of dining in friendly company. Next, the idea of going to the 'Empire' filled her with a certain sense of pained curiosity and excitement. La Marina was the chief attraction there, and she had never seen her. So she shut up her books and papers, put on a simple black skirt, and a pretty blouse of soft pink chiffon, daintily adorned with a shoulder-knot of roses, tied her rich hair up, in the fashion of the picture of Madame le Brun, with a strip of pink ribbon, bade good-bye to Spartan, gave him her glove to guard by way of consolation, and then went with her old friend, leaving for her husband, in case he should return, the brief note that had vexed his high mightiness so seriously. And it was with a strained anticipation and sharp unrest that she sat in the box at the 'Empire,' withdrawn from view as much as possible, and waited for the appearance of the famous dancer, whose performance was advertised on the programme as 'Marvellous Evolution! The Birth of a Butterfly! La Marina!' The music-hall was crowded, and looking down on the densely-packed arena, she saw rows and rows of men, smoking, grinning, whispering in each other's ears,—some sitting squat in their *fauteuils*, with the

MARIE CORELLI

bulging appearance of over-filled flour sacks, the extended feet beyond the sacks, and the apoplectically swelled heads on the tops thereof, suggestive of the full meals just enjoyed,—others, standing up with opera glasses levelled at the promenade, or else leering in the same direction without glasses at all. There were young men, sodden and stupid with smoke and drink,—and old men, blear-eyed and weak-jointed, painfully endeavouring to assume the airs of joyous juvenility. There were fast women, with eyelashes so darkened with kohl as to give them the appearance at a distance of having no eyes at all, but only black sockets;—middle-aged frowsy feminine topers, whose very expression of face intimated a 'looking forward to the next glass,'—and a few almost palsy-stricken antiquities of womanhood, the possible ruins of fifty-year-ago ballet-girls and toe-and-heel stage 'fairies,' who sat in the stalls twisting their poor old mouths into the contortion of a coquettish smile—a contortion dreadfully reminding one of the way a skull grins when some careless gravedigger throws it out of the mould where it has hidden its ghastly mirth for perhaps twenty years. All this seething witches' cauldron of life, Delicia looked down upon with a mingling of shame and sorrow. Were these low-looking creatures real humanity?—the humanity which God created and redeemed? Surely not! They were more like apes than human beings—how was it?—and why was it? She was still pondering the question when old Mr. Cavendish spoke.

'Not a very distinguished audience, is it, Delicia?' he said. He had called her Delicia from childhood, and he did not care, at the age of sixty-five, to break himself of the pleasant habit.

'No,' she replied, with a faint smile; 'I have never been here before. Have you?'

'Oh, yes, often; and so has my wife. The great advantage of music-halls like these is that one can come and be entertained at any moment of the evening without being forced to devour one's dinner with the lightning speed of a Yankee tourist. The mistake made by all theatre managers is the earliness of the hour they appoint for the rising of the curtain. Eight o'clock! Good heavens!—that's the usual London dinner time; and if one wants to get to the theatre punctually one must dine at six-thirty, which is ridiculous. Plays ought to commence at half-past nine and finish at half-past eleven; especially during the season. No man who loves his home comfort cares to gallop through the pleasantest meal of the day, and rush off to a theatre at eight o'clock; it's hard work, and is seldom rewarded by any real pleasure. The "Empire" and other places of the same character get on so very well, partly because they leave us a certain choice of hours. La Marina, you see, doesn't come on till ten.'

'She is very beautiful, isn't she?' asked Delicia.

'Oh, my dear!' said Mrs. Cavendish, laughing a little, 'Beautiful is rather a strong expression! She's a—well—! What would you call her, Robert?' appealing to her husband.

'I should call her a fine, fleshy woman,' answered Mr. Cavendish; 'Coarsely built, certainly; and I should say she drank a good deal. She'll get on all right enough while she's young; but at middle-age she'll be an appalling spectacle in the way of fat!'

He laughed, but Delicia scarcely heard his last words. She was lost in a wondering reverie. She could have easily understood a low-minded man becoming enamoured of an equally low-minded woman, but what puzzled her was to realise that her handsome and proudly-aristocratic husband should find anything attractive in a person who was 'coarse' and 'drank a good deal.' But now the musical prelude to the wonderful 'Birth of a Butterfly' began, and the low shivering of the violins responded to the melodious complaints of the deeper-toned 'cellos, as the lights of the 'Empire' were darkened, and over the crowded audience the kindly veil of a semi-obscurity fell, hiding the play of mean and coarse emotions on many a degraded face, and completely shadowing the wicked devilry of eyes so bereft of honesty, that had hell itself needed fresh sparks to kindle flame, those ugly human glances might have served the purpose. The curtain rose, displaying an exquisitely-painted scene called the 'Garden of Aurora,' where, in the rosy radiance of a deftly-simulated 'dawn of day,' the green trees trembled to the murmur of the subdued orchestral music, and roses—admirable creations of calico and gauze—hung from the wings in gay clusters, looking almost as if they were real. In the middle of the stage, on a broad green leaf that glittered with a thousand sparkles of imitation dew, lay a large golden cocoon, perfect in shape and shining gloriously in the beams of the mimic sun, to this central object the gaze of everyone in the audience was drawn and fixed. The music now grew wilder and sharper, the violins began to scream, the 'cellos to swear, and Sound itself, torn into shreds of impatient vibration, was beginning to protest discordantly at the whole representation, when lo!—the golden cocoon grew slowly more and more transparent, as if some invisible hand were winding off the silken treasure of the spinning, and the white form of a woman was dimly, delicately seen through the half-opaque covering. Loud murmurs of applause began, which swelled into a rapturous roar of ecstasy as with a sudden, sharp noise, which was echoed and repeated in the orchestra, the cocoon split asunder, and La Marina bounded forward to the footlights. Clad in diaphanous drapery, which scarcely concealed her form, and spreading forth two white butterfly wings, illumined in some mysterious way by electricity, she commenced her gliding dance—an intricate whirl of wonderful sinuous movements, every one of which might have served as a study for a sculptor. Her feet moved flyingly without sound; her face, artistically tinted for stage-effect, was beautiful; her hair of reddish-brown, lit weirdly by concealed electric dewdrops, flowed about her in a cloud that resembled a smouldering fire; and as she danced, she smiled as sweetly and with as perfect an imitation of childlike innocence as though she had in very truth been newly born in fairyland that night, just as she seemed,—a creature of light, love and mirth, with no idea at all of the brandy awaiting her by her own order in her dressing-room off the 'wings.' And Delicia, frozen into a kind of unnatural calm, watched her steadily, coldly, critically; and watching, realised that the Bond Street jeweller had not spoken without knowledge, for there, on Marina's panting bosom, gleamed the diamond dove carrying the golden love-token, which said, '*Je t'adore ma mie!*' Flashing brilliantly with every toss and whirl of the dancer's pliant body, it was to Delicia the proof-positive of her husband's dishonour. And yet she found it difficult to grasp the truth at once; she was not aware of any particular emotion of hurt, or rage, or grief; she only felt very cold and sick, and she could not put so strong a control on herself as to quite hide these physical sensations altogether, for Mrs. Cavendish, glancing at her in alarm, exclaimed,—

'Delicia, you are not well! Robert, she's going to faint; take her out of the box! Give her some air!'

Delicia forced herself to smile—to speak.

'It is nothing, I assure you,' she said, 'nothing but the heat and the smoke. Pray do not mind me; it will soon pass.'

But despite her words, she half rose and looked nervously about her as if seeking for some escape; then, refusing Mr. Cavendish's hastily-offered arm, she sat down again.

'I will see this dance out,' she said tremulously; 'and then, perhaps, if you are ready, we will go.'

And she turned her eyes once more on the stage, which was now flooded with purple and golden light, causing La Marina, in her impersonation of a butterfly, to glow with all the brilliant and soft colours of the rainbow. Her white wings were irradiated with all sorts of wonderful tints—now crimson, now blue, now green—and in the midst of all the glitter and play of light shone Marina's face, smiling with its sweetly simulated expression of innocence, while the diamond dove sparkled beneath her rounded chin. And as Delicia glanced from her to the arena to see the effect of the performance on the audience, she started, and in the extreme tension of her nerves almost screamed,—for there,—looking straight up at her, was her husband! Their eyes met; the crowded space of the auditorium and the brilliantly-lit stage, with the swaying figure of the popular dancer gliding to and fro upon it, severed them—the visible and outward signs of a wider separation to come. Lord Carlyon surveyed his wife with a lofty and offended air, and quickly understanding the expression on his features, Delicia could have laughed aloud, had she been less stunned and miserable. For he was assuming an aspect of injured virtue, which, considering the actual state of affairs, had something ludicrous about it; and for a moment Delicia studied him with a curiously calm and critical analysis, just as if he were a subject for literary treatment and no more. She saw, from his very look upward at her, that he considered her to have outraged the proprieties by visiting the 'Empire' at all, even though she was accompanied by two of her oldest and most familiar friends; and of his own guilt in connection with La Marina it was highly probable he never thought at all. Men are judged to be excellent logicians, superseding in that particular branch of knowledge all the feeble efforts of womankind; and undoubtedly they have a very peculiar form of arguing out excuses for their own vices, which must be acknowledged as exceedingly admirable. Before La Marina's gyrations were over, and while the male part of the audience was exhausting itself in frantic salvos of applause, Delicia was moved by such a keen and pungent appreciation of the comedy side of the situation that she could not help smiling. There was a wide wound in her heart; but it was so deep and deadly that as yet the true anguish of it was not betrayed—the throbbing ache had not begun, and she herself was scarcely as yet aware of her own mortal hurt. The brilliancy of her brain saved her, for the time being, from knowing to what extent her tenderest and best emotions had been outraged; and she could not avoid perceiving something almost droll in the fact that she, Delicia, had worked, among other things, for this, to enable her husband to deck his mistress with jewels purchased out of her hard earnings!

'It is very funny!' she said half aloud, 'and perhaps the funniest thing of all is that I should never have thought it of him!'

'What did you say, Delicia?' asked Mr. Cavendish, bending down towards her.

Delicia smiled.

'Nothing!' she replied. 'I was talking to myself, which is a bad habit. I saw Will just now; he's in the arena somewhere. I expect he's not best pleased to see me here.'

'Well, he's here himself often enough,' retorted Mr. Cavendish; 'at least, if one is to believe what people say.'

'Ah, but one must never believe what people say,' answered Delicia, still smiling quite radiantly. 'The majority of mankind tell more lies than truths; it suits their social customs and conveniences better. May we go now?'

'Willingly,' and the Cavendishes rose at once. 'Shall we look for Lord Carlyon?'

'Oh, no; there is such a crowd, we should never find him. He will probably go home in a hansom.'

They left the hall; and Delicia, who had placed her carriage at the service of her friends that night, took them back in it to their own door.

'You haven't told us what you think of La Marina,' said Mrs. Cavendish, smiling, when they were bidding each other good-night. 'Were you disappointed in her?'

'Not at all,' Delicia answered tranquilly; 'she is an admirable dancer. I never expected her to be anything more than that.'

'Numbers of men have quite lost their heads about her,' observed Mr. Cavendish, as he stood on the pavement outside his house and looked in at Delicia, where she sat in her carriage shadowed from the light. 'Somebody told me the other day she had more jewels than a queen.'

'No doubt,' responded Delicia, carelessly; 'She is a toy, and the only chance she has of not being broken is to make herself expensive. Good-night!'

She waved her hand, and was driven off. Mr. and Mrs. Cavendish entered their own quiet house, and in the semi-lighted hall looked at each other questioningly.

'It is no use dropping any more casual hints,' said Mr. Cavendish, almost crossly; 'she doesn't take them.'

'I don't think she'll ever believe a word against Carlyon,' responded his wife; 'and old friends as we are, we should only offend her if we speak out and tell her all we hear. It is no use making mischief.'

'It is no use speaking truth, you mean,' observed Mr. Cavendish. 'What a singular thing it is that one can never be honest in society without offending somebody!'

Mrs. Cavendish sighed and smiled. She had had her turn of social life long years ago, and had got thoroughly tired of its vapid folly and hypocrisy, but she had managed to find a good husband, and for that was daily and hourly thankful. The great sorrow of her life was that she had not been blessed with children, and it was partly this shadow, on her otherwise happy and tranquil lot, which made her attachment to Delicia peculiarly tender. Had that brilliant and popular novelist been her own daughter, she could not have loved her more, and there was an uneasy sense of foreboding in her good, motherly soul that night which kept her awake for a long time, thinking and wondering as to what would happen if certain rumours concerning Lord Carlyon turned out to be true. She knew Delicia's character better than most people; she was aware that beneath that apparently pliant, sweet nature, there was a resolute spirit, strong as iron, firm as adamant—a spirit which would assuredly make for right and justice whenever and however tested and tried; but she could not foresee in what way Delicia would resent a wrong, supposing she had cause for such resentment. She looked slight as a reed and delicate as a lily; but appearances are deceptive; and nothing can well be more foolish than to estimate a person's mental capacity by his or her outward bearing. A rapier is a thin, light weapon, but it can nevertheless kill; a nightingale has nothing to boast of in its plumage, but its singing surpasses that of all the other birds in creation. Only the purely barbaric mind judges things or individuals by surface appearances. Anyone who had attempted to fathom Delicia's character by her looks would have formed a very erroneous estimate of her, for, to the casual observer, she was merely a pretty, lovable woman, with a sunny smile and a graceful bearing, and that was all. No one would have given her credit for such virtues as strong self-restraint, courage, determination, and absolute indifference to opinions; yet all these she had in no small degree, combined with an extraordinary directness and swiftness of action which is commendable enough when it distinguishes a man, but is somewhat astonishing when discovered in the naturally capricious composition of a woman. This direct method of conduct

MARIE CORELLI

impelled her now; for while Mrs. Cavendish lay awake worrying about her, she herself, on returning home that evening, had fully made up her mind as to what she meant to do. Going into her study, she sat down and wrote a letter to her husband, in which, with concise and uncomplaining brevity, she told him all. She concluded her epistle thus:—

'I am unable to tell you my own feelings on this matter, as I have not yet had time to realise them even to myself. The surprise is too sudden—the disappointment I experience in you too keen. I am quite aware that many men keep stage-artistes for their own amusement in hours of leisure, but I do not think they are accustomed to do so on their wives' earnings. It would be inexpressibly painful to me to have to talk this over with you; it is a subject I could not possibly discuss. I therefore deem it best to leave you for a few days in order that we may both, apart from one another, have leisure in which to consider our positions and arrange what is best to do for the future. In order to save all unnecessary gossip and scandal, I shall return to town in time for Lady Dexter's "crush," to which we are both especially invited. I am going to Broadstairs, and will telegraph my address on arrival.

DELICIA VAUGHAN

When she had written all she had to say, she placed the letter in an envelope, addressed it, and, calling Robson, bade him deliver it to his master directly he returned. Robson glanced at her deferentially, wondering within himself at the extreme pallor of her face and feverish brightness of her eyes.

'His lordship said he would probably not return to-night,' he ventured to observe.

Delicia started slightly, but quickly controlled herself.

'Did he? Well, whenever he does return, give him that letter.'

'Yes, my lady.'

He withdrew, and Delicia went quietly upstairs to her bedroom and summoned her maid.

'I am going down to the sea for a few days, Emily,' she said; 'to Broadstairs. Just put my things together, and be ready yourself by ten o'clock to-morrow morning.'

Emily, a bright-looking young woman, who had none of the airs and graces about her which are too frequently assumed by ladies' maids, and who, moreover, had the further recommendation of being devotedly attached to her mistress, received her instructions with her usual pleased readiness, and set about loosening her lady's hair for the night. As she unwound the glistening mass and let it fall, Delicia suddenly started up with a smothered cry of pain.

'Oh, my lady, what is it?' exclaimed Emily, startled.

Delicia stood trembling and looking at her.

'Nothing, nothing,' she faltered at last, faintly forcing a smile. 'I have just found out something, that is all—something I did not quite understand before. I understand it now—I understand—my God, I understand! There, Emily, don't look so frightened. I am not ill; I am only a little tired and puzzled. You can go now; I would rather be alone. Be sure you call me in good time for the train, and have everything packed in readiness. I shall take Spartan with me.'

'Yes, my lady,' stammered Emily, still looking a trifle scared. 'Are you sure you are not ill? Can't I do anything for you?'

'No, nothing,' answered Delicia, gently. 'Go to bed, Emily, and get up early, that's all. Good-night!'

'Good-night, my lady!' and Emily reluctantly retired.

Left alone, Delicia moved to the door and locked it. Then, turning, she drew aside the curtain which hung before the niche she called her 'oratory,' where an ivory crucifix hung white against draperies of purple. The anguished eyes of the suffering Saviour looked down upon her; the thorn-crowned head drooped as it were towards her; the 'Man of Sorrows acquainted with grief,' with arms outstretched upon the cross, seemed waiting to receive her,—and with a sudden, sobbing cry she fell on her knees.

'Oh, my God, my God.' she wailed, 'I know now what I have lost! All my love and all my joy! Gone, gone like a foolish dream,—gone for ever! Gone, and nothing left but the crown of thorns called Fame!'

Shuddering, she hid her face on the cushion of her *prie-dieu* and wept slow, passionate tears, that rose from a breaking heart and scalded her eyelids as they fell. Veiled in the golden glory of her hair, she fretted like a little ailing child, till finally, exhausted and shivering with emotion, she lifted her head and looked straight at the sculptured Christ that faced her.

'I have loved him too much,' she said half aloud. 'I have made him the idol of my life, and I am punished for my sin. We are all apt to forget the thunders of Mount Sinai and the great Voice which said, "Thou shalt have none other gods save Me." I had forgotten,—nay, I was almost willing to forget! I made of my beloved a god; he has made of me—a convenience!'

She rose, flung back her hair over her shoulders, and standing still for a moment listened. There was not a sound in the house, save an occasional uneasy movement from Spartan, who was lying on his mat outside her bedroom door.

"'My lord's' sense of what is right and proper for women has been outraged to-night by seeing me at the "Empire," she said, with a little disdainful smile; 'but his notions of morality do not go far enough to prevent him from being with La Marina at this very moment!'

A look of disgust passed over her mobile features.

'Poor Love! Poor little, delicate moth! How soon a coarse touch will kill it—kill it hopelessly, so that it will never rise again! It is the only passion I think we possess that once dead, can never be resuscitated. Ambition is perennial, but Love!—it is the aloe flower that blossoms but once in a hundred years. I wonder what I shall do with my life now,—now that it is crippled and paralysed?'

She walked slowly to her mirror and looked long and earnestly at her own reflection.

'You poor little woman!' she said pityingly, 'What a mistake you have made of it! You fancied that out of all the world of men you had won for yourself a hero,—a man whose nature was noble, whose disposition was chivalrous, whose tenderness and truth were never to be doubted! A protector and defender who, had anyone presumed to slander you, would have struck the liar across the mouth and made him answer for his insolence. Instead of this wonderful Marc Antony or Theseus of your imagination, what have you got? Don't be afraid, poor Delicia! I see your mouth trembling and your eyes filling with foolish tears— now that's all nonsense, you know! You must not shrink from the truth, my dear; and if God has chosen to take up your beautiful idol and break it in your sight, you must not begin to argue about it, or try to pick up the pieces and tell God He is wrong. Courage, Delicia! Face it out! What did you think you had won for a sure certainty out of all the flitting pageant of this world's illusions? A true heart,—a faithful lover,—and, as before said, a kind of Theseus in looks and bravery! But even Theseus deserted Ariadne, and in this case your hero has deserted you. Only what you have to realise, you deluded creature, is this—that he is not a hero at all—that he never was a hero! That is the hardest part, isn't it? To think that the god you have worshipped is no more than an "officer and gentleman," as a great many "officers and gentlemen" go, who lives comfortably on your earnings, and spends the surplus money on the race-course, music-halls and—La Marina! Put off your rose-coloured spectacles, my dear, and look at him as he is. Don't be a little coward about it! Yes, I know what you are saying over and over again in your own heart; it is the old story, "I loved him, oh, I loved him!" like the burden of a sentimental song. Of course you loved him—how deeply,—how passionately,—how dearly,—you will never, never be able to express, even to yourself.'

Here, in spite of her remonstrances to her own image in the glass, the tears brimmed over and fell.

'There, of course I suppose you must cry a little; you can't help it,— you have been so thoroughly deceived, and the disillusion is so complete, you poor, poor little woman!'

And, moved by a quaint compassion for herself, she leant forward and kissed the reflection of her own quivering lips in the mirror.

'It's no good your looking about anywhere for consolation,' she went on, wiping away her tears. 'You are not made after the fashion of the modern lady, who can love anywhere and everywhere, so large is her heart; you are of that dreadfully old-world type of person, who, loving once, can never love again. Your love is killed in you; you are only half yourself now, and you must make the best of it. You must cut down your sentiments, smother your emotions, and live like St. John in the wilderness, on 'locusts and wild honey,' by which you will for the future understand the rewards of Fame. And you will be in a desert all by yourself, fasting—fasting day and night—for the food of tenderness and love which you will never, never get—remember that! It's rather a hard lot, you poor, weeping, weak little woman! But it's marked out for you, and you will have to bear it!'

She smiled a pained, difficult smile, and she watched her own reflection smile back at her in the same sad way. Glancing at a time-piece on her dressing-table, she saw it was nearly two in the morning. Her husband had not returned. Twisting up her hair in a loose knot, she lay down on the bed and tried to sleep, but only succeeded in falling into an uneasy doze for about an hour. Ill and restless as she felt, however, she was up and dressed when her maid came to her in the morning,

MARIE CORELLI

and before eleven o'clock she had left the house, with Spartan sitting beside her on the floor of the brougham which took her to the station, from whence she started for Broadstairs. She left no instructions with her household, beyond impressing once again upon Robson the urgent necessity of giving Lord Carlyon the letter she had written for him as soon as he returned. Robson promised implicit obedience, and watched the disappearance of the carriage containing his lady, her maid and her dog, with feelings of mingled curiosity and uneasiness.

'Something's in the wind, I'm pretty sure,' he mused; 'she has never gone away in this way, sudden-like, before. Very quiet, too, she looks, and very pale. She wouldn't be the one to make a fuss about anything, but she'd feel all the more. I wonder if she knows?'

He stopped abruptly in the middle of the hall, evidently struck by this idea, and repeated the words to himself slowly and reflectively—'I wonder if she knows?'

VII

It is strange, but nevertheless true, despite all our latter-day efforts at the reasoning away of sentiment, that conscience is still so very much alive in some of us, that when a man of birth and good-breeding has, according to his own stock-phrase for indulgence in vicious amusements, 'seen life,' by spending his time in low company, he is frequently moved by a strong reaction,—so powerful as almost to create nausea, and put him in a very bad and petulant humour. This was the case with Carlyon when he returned to his home at about luncheon time on the day Delicia departed seawards. He was not merely irritable, but he took a fantastic pleasure in knowing himself to be irritable, and in keeping his temper up to the required pitch of spleen. He was really angry with himself, but he managed to pretend that he was angry with Delicia. He had seen something in one of the papers about her which he judged as quite sufficient ground of offence to go upon, though he knew it was an attempt to vilify her fair name, which he, as her husband, should have instantly resented. In his own mind he was perfectly cognisant that, had he acted a manly part in the matter, he should have taken his riding-whip, and with it dealt a smart cut across the face of the literary liar who had published the false rumour, and yet, though he was aware of this, he had managed to work himself up into such a peculiar condition of self-pity that he could see nothing at all on his limited horizon but himself, his own feelings and his own perfections; and though he was partially and shamedly conscious of his own vices as well, he found such a number of excuses for these, that by the time he reached his own door he had, by dint of many soothing modern doctrines, and comfortable progressive moralist arguments, almost decided that he, taking men as they were, was really an exceptional paragon and pattern of virtue.

'I must really speak very seriously to Delicia,' he said to himself. 'A woman as well-known as she is ought not to be seen at the "Empire," and she has no business to receive actors at her "at homes."'

With these highly moral feelings at work within him, he admitted himself into his own house, or rather his wife's house, with his latch-key, and finding no one about, walked straight upstairs into Delicia's study. The blinds were down, the room was deserted, and only the marble 'Antinous' stared at him with a cold smile. Descending to the hall again, he summoned Robson, who, instantly appearing, handed him Delicia's letter on a silver salver with elaborately polite ceremony.

'What's this?' he asked impatiently. 'Is her ladyship out again?'

'She left for Broadstairs this morning, my lord,' replied Robson, demurely. 'Her maid went with her, and she took Spartan.'

Carlyon muttered something like an oath, and turning into the smoking-room, opened and read his wife's letter. Growing hot and cold by turns, he perused every calm, convincing, clearly-written word, and for a moment sat stunned and completely overwhelmed. Guilt, shame and remorse fought for the mastery of his feelings, and during the space of two or three minutes he thought he would at once follow Delicia, throw himself on her mercy, declare everything, and ask her forgiveness. But what would be the use of that? She might forgive, but she would never forget. And her blind adoration of him, her passionate love, her devout confidence? He had sense enough to realise that these fair feelings of tenderness and reverence in her for him were dead for ever!

Pulling at his handsome moustache fretfully, he surveyed his position and wondered whether it was likely that she would sue for a divorce? And if so, would she get it? No, for she could not prove cruelty or desertion. There was no cruelty in his having an 'affair' with Marina, or a dozen Marinas if he liked—*not in the eyes of the law*. There was not even any cruelty, legally speaking, in his spending his wife's earnings on Marina, if his wife gave him money to do as he liked with. To get a divorce legally, Delicia would have to prove not only infidelity but cruelty and desertion as well for two years and upwards. Oh, just law! Made by men for themselves and their own convenience! The 'cruelty' which robs an innocent woman of love, of confidence, of happiness at one blow, has no existence, according to masculine justice. She may have to endure wilful neglect, and to be the witness of the open intimacy of her husband with other women; but provided he does not beat her, or otherwise physically ill-use her, and continues to live with her in apparent union, while all the while she shrinks from his touch and resents his companionship as an outrage, she cannot be separated from him. This Carlyon remembered with a commendable amount of self-congratulation.

'She can't get rid of me, that's one thing,' he reflected; 'not that I suppose she would try it on. Damn that Bond Street jeweller for an ass! Why couldn't the fellow hold his confounded tongue! Of course, it is a split between us; but, by Jove!—a woman who writes books ought to know that a man must get some fun out of life. We can't all be literary!

Besides, if there is to be a row, I have got a very good cause of complaint on my side!'

Whereupon he snatched up a pen and wrote as follows:—

DEAR DELICIA,

I regret that a woman of your culture and intelligence should not be able to understand the world and the ways of the world better. Men do not discuss such subjects as that alluded to in your letter; the least said the soonest mended. I enclose a cutting from *Honesty*, in which you will perceive that I possibly have more cause to complain of you than you of me. Greater licence is permitted to men than to women, as I imagined you knew, and your position with regard to the public should make you doubly careful. I hope you will enjoy your change of air.

Yours affectionately,
WILL

He read over the press-cutting alluded to, which ran as follows:—

'It has been frequently rumoured that the real "Dona Sol" of the "Ernani" who has been so long delighting the histrionic world, is a well-known lady novelist, who has been lifted into far more prominence that her literary capabilities would ever have given her, by her marriage into the aristocracy with a certain gallant Guards officer. The "Dona" in question has long been considered "as chaste as ice, as pure as snow," but ice and snow are prone to melt in the heat of an ardent passion, and the too evident ardour of the "Ernani" in this case has, we hear, won him his cause, with the result that the "ears of the groundlings" will shortly be tickled with a curious scandal.'

'After all,' muttered Carlyon, as he thrust this in an envelope, 'it's much worse that she, as a woman, should be coupled with Paul Valdis, than that I as a man should amuse myself with Marina. She is ridiculously inconsistent; she ought to know that a man in this world does as he likes,—a woman does as she must. The two things are totally different. Now, I shall have to wait till she telegraphs her address before I can send this. What an infernal nuisance!'

MARIE CORELLI

He betook himself to his usual consolation—a cigar and puffed away at it crossly, wondering what he should do with himself. He was sick of La Marina for the time being—there were no race-meetings on, and he felt that to be thus left to his own resources was a truly unkind dispensation of Providence. He had a very limited brain capacity, his one idea of life being to get amusement out of it somehow. Perpetual amusement is apt to tire; but of this the votaries of so-called pleasure never think, till they are flung back upon themselves exhausted. Carlyon would have been in his right place had he been born as a noble of high rank in ancient Pompeii—going to the baths, having his hair combed and his garments scented; wearing fresh chaplets of flowers round his neck, being fed on the rarest delicacies and drinking the costliest wines, and dividing his affections between several of the prettiest dancing girls. Such an existence would have suited him perfectly, and it is quite possible that when Vesuvius blazed forth its convincing representation of the Day of Judgment, he would have fronted his fate with the stern composure of the immortal 'Roman soldier'; for it is precisely such pampered persons who are the best possible food for flame, or powder and shot; and who generally, as though moved by some instinctive perception of the worthlessness of their lives to the world, meet death with equanimity.

In the interim, while her husband was preparing what he considered a Parthian shot for her in the way of the press-cutting from the society scandal bill called *Honesty*, Delicia had, by the merest chance, bought the paper and read the paragraph on her way down to Broadstairs. She was a woman who never wasted time about anything, and on arriving at her destination she enclosed the paper in an envelope to her lawyers, with the brief instruction appended—:

'Insist on immediate retraction and apology. If refused, take proceedings.'

This done, she dismissed the matter from her mind with a quickness which would have been impossible to any woman who was not absolutely innocent of wrong-doing. A clear conscience is never disturbed by outside slanders, and a straightforward life is never thrust out of its clean onward course by a scandalmonger's sneer. Besides, Delicia's thoughts were too much occupied with her broken idols to dwell long on any other subject of contemplation. All she desired for the moment was rest—a space of silence in which to think calmly and to brace her spirit up to the necessary fortitude required for the realisation of what she must expect to endure for the remainder of her life. She took some quiet rooms facing the sea, telegraphed her address to her husband, and then prepared to settle down for a few days of serious meditation. She began to consider her position with a logical steadiness worthy of any and all or her 'dear old Pagans,' as she called Socrates and the rest of his school,—and with a mingling of timidity and resolve tried the measure of her feminine strength, as a warrior might try his weapon, against the opposing evils which confronted her. The greatest loss that can befall a woman had befallen her—the loss of love. Her love had been deep and passionate, but the object of that love had proved himself unworthy—hence love was dead and would never revive again. This was the first clause of the argument, and it had to be mastered thoroughly. Next came the fact that, notwithstanding the death of love, she, Delicia, was bound to the corpse of that perished passion—bound by the marriage tie and also by the law, which has generously provided that a husband may be guilty of infidelity to his wife every day and every hour of the day, without her having any right to punish or to leave him unless he treats her with 'cruelty,' his unfaithfulness not being judged by the so admirable law as 'cruel.' By no means—oh, no!—not at all! When it comes to blows, face-scratching and hair-tearing, then 'cruelty' can be complained of; but the slow breaking of a heart, the torturing of delicate nerve-fibres on the rack of mental and moral outrage, the smile which is an insult, the condescending tolerance which is an affront, the conventional keeping up of appearances which is a daily lie—all this has no touch of 'cruelty' at all about it—not in the very least!

'Therefore,' argued Delicia, with a fine disdain, 'unless he ever takes it into his head to beat me, or fire a pistol at me, I have no cause of complaint against him, and must not complain. Then must I play the hypocrite and pretend to worship him still? No! That I cannot do; that I will not do. Perhaps he will agree to a separation—' she paused and her face darkened; 'if I make it financially worth his while!'

It was the evening of her arrival at Broadstairs, and she was walking along by the shore, Spartan pacing majestically beside her. The after-glow of the sunken sun rested on the calm sea, and little waves, dimpling one over the other in long, fine lines, broke on the pebbly beach with a soft sound as of children's laughter. Everything was very peaceful and

MARIE CORELLI

beautiful, and by degrees her troubled mind became soothed and gently attuned to the symphonic vibrations of the eternal pulse of Nature for ever beating in answer to the voice of God. Some strong emotion in her own soul suddenly stirred and spoke as it were aloud in accents half-reproachful, half-consoling.

'What is it you have lost?' demanded the inward voice. 'Love? But what do you understand by love? The transitory gleam of light that falls upon a fleck of foam and passes? Or the eternal glory of a deepening day whose summer splendours shall not cease? All that is of the earth must perish; choose therefore that which is of Heaven, and for which you were destined when God kindled first within your woman's soul the fires of aspiration and endeavour! Nature is unrolled before you like an open book; humanity, with all its sufferings, needs and hopes, is here for you to help and comfort; self is a nothing in what you have to do; your earthly good, your earthly love, your earthly hopes are as the idle wind in the countings of eternity! Sail by the compass of the Spirit of God within you; and haply out of darkness, light shall come!'

With dreamy, half-tearful eyes she looked out upon the darkening sea; the sense or a great solitude, a vast loneliness, encompassed her; and almost in unconscious appeal she laid her small, delicate, bare hand on Spartan's shaggy head, who received the caress with a worshipping reverence in his brown eyes.

'It is so hard, Spartan!' she murmured, 'So hard for a woman to be quite alone in the world! To work on, solitary, wearing a bitter laurel-crown that makes one's brow ache; to be deprived, for no fault of one's own, of all the kisses and endearments so freely bestowed on foolish, selfish, ungrateful, and frequently unchaste women—to be set apart in the cold Courts of Fame,—a white statue, with frozen lips and eyes staring down the illimitable ways of Death—Oh God! is not an hour of love worth all this chill renown!'

Tears sprang to her eyes and blotted out the view of the darkening heavens and quiet sea. She turned blindly to move onward, when Spartan suddenly sprang forward with a deep bark of pleasure, and a man's voice, low, and trembling with emotion, said hastily,—

'Lady Carlyon, may I speak to you? I came after you from town. I thought I should find you here!'

And looking up amazed, she found herself face to face with Paul Valdis.

VIII

For a moment she could not speak; astonishment and a lurking sense of indignation held her mute. He meanwhile caressing and endeavouring to soothe Spartan, who frolicked about him in an uncouth dance of joy, went on quickly,—.

'I have followed you. I wanted to tell you all. Yesterday afternoon I saw that paragraph in *Honesty*; and last night I thrashed the writer of it within an inch of his life!'

She raised her eyes with a faint, deprecating smile.

'Yes,' he continued, with an involuntary clenching of his hands, 'I wish all the dirty scandalmongers of the Press were as sore and thoroughly well bruised as he is to-day! This morning I went to the editor of the paper on which he chiefly works, and told him the true character of the man he was employing, and how, under the name of "Brown" he was writing himself up in the press as the "poet" Aubrey Grovelyn, and a complete exposure of the rascal will be published to-morrow. This done, I drove straight to your house. The servants told me you had left early for Broadstairs, and that Lord Carlyon was out. Acting on an impulse, I came after you. We are preparing for a new piece at my theatre, as I daresay you have heard, and I am just now at comparative leisure. I knew nothing of your address, but this is a little place, and I imagined I should find you somewhere by the sea.'

He stopped abruptly, almost breathlessly, looking at her with a world of speechless anxiety in his eyes. She met his gaze with a most untroubled calm.

'I am afraid I do not quite understand you, Mr. Valdis,' she said gently. 'What is it you are speaking of? The paragraph in *Honesty*? I have not given it a thought, I assure you, except to send it to my lawyers. They will know exactly what to do on my behalf. You have troubled yourself about it most needlessly. It is very good of you; but I thought you knew I never paid the slightest attention to what the journals say of me. They may call me a black woman, or a Cherokee squaw for all I care, and they may endow me with a dozen husbands and fifty grandchildren—I should never take the trouble to contradict them!' She laughed a little, then regarded him intently. 'You look quite ill. What have you been doing with yourself? Don't imagine I am angry with you for coming—I am delighted. I was just beginning to feel very lonely and to wish I had a friend.'

Her lip trembled suspiciously, but she turned her head aside that he might not see the emotion in her face.

'I have always been your friend,' said Valdis, huskily, 'but—you were offended with me.'

She sighed.

'Oh, yes, I was! I am not now. Circumstances alter cases, you know. I did not want to look bad fortune in the face till I was forced to do so, and I resented your attempt to tear the bandage from my eyes. But it's all right now—I am no longer blind. I wish I were!'

'It is my turn to say I don't understand,' said Valdis, wonderingly. 'I thought you would naturally be as annoyed at that insolent paragraph as I was—and I took instant means to punish—'

'Oh, the paragraph again!' murmured Delicia, wearily. 'What does it matter? If the newspapers said you were me, or I were you, or that we had been married and separated, or that we danced a hornpipe together on the sly whenever we could get a chance, why should we care? Who that has any common sense cares for the half-crown or five-shilling paragraphist? And who, having brains at all, pays any attention to society journalism?'

'Brains or no brains,' said Valdis, hotly, 'it does one good to thrash a liar now and then, whether he be in journalism or out of it, and I have given Mr. Brown, *alias* Aubrey Grovelyn, good cause to remember me this time. I only hope he'll have sufficient spirit left to summon me for assault, that I may defend myself and state openly in a court of justice what a precious rascal he is!'

'Aubrey Grovelyn!' echoed Delicia, with a half smile, 'why, that's the man the press has been "booming" lately, isn't it? Calling him a "second Shakespeare and Milton combined?" Oh, dear! And you have actually beaten this marvel of the ages!'

She began to laugh—the natural vivacity of her nature asserted itself for a moment, and her face lightened with all that brilliant animation which gave it its chiefest charm. Valdis looked at her, and, despite the heat of his own conflicting emotions, smiled.

'Yes, I have beaten him like a dog,' he responded, 'though why I should do the noble race to which Spartan belongs, a wrong by mentioning it in connection with a creature like Grovelyn, I do not know. Spartan, old boy, I ask your pardon! The booming you speak of, Lady Carlyon, has in every instance been done by Grovelyn himself. It is he and he alone who has styled himself "Shakespeare and Milton *redivivus*," and his self-log-rolling scheme was so cunningly devised that it was rather difficult to find him out. But I have been on the watch some time, and have hunted him down at last. He has been on the staff of the *Daily Chanticleer* for two years as Alfred Brown, and in that character has managed to work up "a new poet" in Aubrey Grovelyn, the said Aubrey Grovelyn being himself. I understand, however, that it is not at all an original idea on his part; the same thing has been and is being done by several other fellows like him. But you are not listening, Lady Carlyon. I suppose I am boring you—'

'Not at all,' and Delicia turned her eyes upon him kindly; 'and you mistake,—I was listening very attentively. I was thinking what miserable tricks and mean devices some people will stoop to in order to secure notoriety. I do not speak of fame—fame is a different thing, much harder to win, much heavier to bear.'

Her voice sank into a melancholy cadence, and Valdis studied her delicate profile in the darkening light with passionate tenderness in his eyes. But he did not speak, and after a little pause she went on dreamily, more to herself than to him,—

'Notoriety is a warm, noisy thing—personified, it is like a fat, comfortable woman who comes into your rooms perspiring, laughing, talking with all the gossip of the town at her tongue's end, who folds you in her arms whether you like it or not, and tells you you are a "dear," and wants to know where you get your gowns made and what you had for dinner—the very essence of broad and vulgar good humour! Fame is like a great white angel, who points you up to a cold, sparkling, solitary mountain-top away from the world, and bids you stay there alone, with the chill stars shining down on you. And people look up at you and pass; you are too far off for the clasp of friendship; you are too isolated for the caress of love; and your enemies, unable to touch you, stare insolently, smile and cry aloud, "So you have climbed to the summit at last! Well, much good may it do you! Stay there, live there, and die there, as you must, alone for ever!" And I think it is hard to be alone, don't you?'

Her words were tremulous, and Valdis saw tears in her eyes. They had wandered on unconsciously, and were close to the pier, which was deserted save for the weather-beaten old mariner, who sat in his little box at the entrance waiting for the pennies that were rather slow in coming in at that particular time of year. Valdis passed himself and his companion through the turn-stile, and they walked side by side on towards the solemn shadows of the murmuring sea.

'Now that we have a few minutes together, you can surely tell me what it is that has gone wrong with you, Lady Carlyon,' he said, his rich voice softening to a great tenderness. 'I am your friend, as you know. I imagined that your displeasure at that paragraph in *Honesty* would have been very great, and justly so; but I begin to fear it is something more serious that makes you seem so unlike yourself—'

She interrupted him by a light touch on his arm.

'Is that true? Do you find me changed?'

And she raised her eyes trustingly to his. He met that confiding look for a moment, then turned away lest the deep love of his soul should be betrayed.

'You are not changed in appearance—no!' he said slowly, 'You are always lovely. But there is a great sadness in your face. I cannot help seeing that.'

She laughed a little, then sighed.

'I should have made a very bad actress,' she said; 'I cannot put a complete disguise on my thoughts. You are right; I am sad; as sad as any woman can be in the world. I have lost my husband's love.'

He started.

'You have heard all, then;—you know?'

She stopped in her walk and faced him steadily.

'What! is it common gossip?' she asked. 'Does all the town chatter of what I, till a few days ago, was ignorant of? If so, then, alas! poor Delicia!'

Her eyes flashed suddenly.

'Tell me, is it possible that Lord Carlyon has so far forgotten himself as to make his attentions to La Marina open and manifest, thus allowing his wife to become an object for the pity and mockery of society?'

'Lady Carlyon,' replied Valdis, 'your friends sought to warn you long ago, but you would not listen. Your own nature, pure and lofty as it is, rejected what you deemed mere scandalous rumour. You resented with the noble confidence of a true wife the least word of suspicion against Lord Carlyon. When I ventured to hint that your confidence was misplaced, you dismissed me from your presence. I do not say you were wrong; you were right. The worthy wife of a worthy husband is bound to act as you did. But suppose the husband is not worthy, and the wife deceives herself as to his merits, it is for her own sake, for her honour and her self-respect that she should be persuaded to realise the fact and take such steps as may prevent her from occupying a false position. And now you know—'

'Now I know,' interrupted Delicia, with a vibrating passion in her voice, 'what is the use of it? What am I to do? What can I do? A woman is powerless in everything which relates to her husband's infidelity merely. I can show no bruises, no evidence of ill-treatment; then what is my complaint about? "Go home, silly woman," says the law, "and understand that if your husband chooses to have a new love every day, you cannot get separated from him, provided he is civil to you; man has licence which woman has not." And so on, and so on, with their eternal jargon! Paul Valdis, you can act emotions and look tragedies; but have you ever realised the depth or the terror of the dumb, dreadful dramas of a woman's broken heart? No! I don't think that even you, with all your fine, imaginative sympathy, can reach thus far. Do you know why I came away from home to-day and made straight for the sea,—the great, calm sea which I knew would have the gentleness to drown me if the pain became too bitter to bear? Nay, do not hold me!' For Valdis, struck by the complete breakdown of her reserve, and the brilliant wildness of her eyes, had unconsciously caught her arm. 'There is no danger, I assure you. I have not been given my faith in God quite vainly; and there is so much of God's thought in the beauty of ocean, that even to contemplate it has made me quieter and stronger; I shall not burden it with my drifting body yet! But do you know, can you guess why I came here and avoided meeting my husband to-day?'

Valdis shook his head, profoundly moved himself by her strong emotion.

'Lest I should kill him!' she said in a thrilling whisper. 'I was afraid of myself! I thought that if I had to see him enter my room with that confident smile of his, that easy manner, that grace of a supreme conceit swaying his every movement, while I all the time knew the fraud he was practising on me, the hypocrisy of his embrace, the lie of his kiss on my lips, I might, in the rush of remembering how I had loved him, murder him! It was possible; I knew it; I realised it; I confessed it before God as a sin; but despite of prayer and confession, the devil's thought remained!—I might do it in a moment of fury,—in a moment when wronged love clamoured for vengeance and would listen to no appeal,—and so I fled from temptation; but now I think the sea and air have absorbed all my evil desires, for they have gone!—and I shall try to be content now, content with solitude, till I die!'

Valdis was still silent. She leant over the pier, looking dreamily down into the darkly-heaving sea.

'Life at best is such a little thing!' she said, 'One wonders sometimes what it is all for! You see crowds of men and women rushing hither and thither, building this thing, destroying that, scheming, contriving, studying, fretting, working, courting, marrying, bringing up their children, and it is quite appalling to think that the same old road has been travelled over and over again since the very beginning! All through the Ptolemies and the Cæsars,—imagine! Exactly the same old monotonous course of human living and dying! What a waste it seems! Optimists say we have progressed; but then are we sure of that? And then one wants to know where the progression leads to; if we are going forward, what *is* the "forward?" Myself, I think the great charm of life is love; without love life is really almost valueless, and surely not worth the trouble of preserving. Don't you agree with me?'

She looked up, and, looking, saw his eyes filled with such an intensity of misery as touched and startled her. He made a slight gesture of appeal.

'For God's sake, don't speak to me like this!' he whispered; 'You torture me!'

She still gazed at him, half wondering, half fearing. He was silent for a few minutes, then resumed slowly in quiet tones.

'You are so candid in your own nature that you can neither wear a disguise yourself nor see when it is worn by others,' he said; 'and just as you have never suspected your husband of infidelity, you have never suspected me—of love. I suppose you, with the majority, have looked upon me as merely the popular mime of the moment, feigning passions I cannot feel, and dividing what purely human emotions my life allows me still to enjoy, among the light wantons of the stage, who rejoice in a multitude of lovers. It is possible you would never believe me capable of a deep and lasting love for any woman?'

He paused,—and Delicia spoke softly and with great gentleness, moved by the strength of her own grief to compassionate his, whatever it might be.

'Indeed I would, Mr. Valdis,' she said earnestly. 'I am quite sure you have a strong and steadfast nature, and that with you it would be a case of "once love, love always."'

He met her eyes fully.

'Thank you,' he said in low accents; 'I am glad you do me that justice. It moves me to make full confession, and to tell you what I thought would never be told. Others, I fear, have guessed my secret, but you—you have never seen it, never guessed it. You are not vain enough to realise your own charm; you live like an angel in a land of divine dreams, and so you have never known that I—I—'

But she suddenly started away from him, her eyes filling with tears, her hands thrust out to keep him back from her.

'No, no,' she cried, 'you must not say it; you must not!'

'Nay, I must and will,' said Valdis, now losing a little of his hard self-control, for he sprang to her side and seized her two hands in his. 'You have guessed it at last, then? That I love you, Delicia! Love you with all my soul, with every breath of my being, every beat of my heart! I have tried to hide it from you; I have battled against my own passion, and the fight has been hard; but when you say—oh, God! with what piteousness in your dear voice—that without love life is valueless, you break down my strength; you make me helpless in your hands, and you unman me! You need not be afraid of me, nor indignant, for I know all you would say. You will never love me; your whole heart was given to one man, your husband; he has flung away the precious gift as though it were naught, and it is broken, dear, quite broken! I know that even better than you do. Such a nature as yours can never love twice. And I know, too, that your proud, pure soul resents my love as an outrage because you are married, though your marriage itself has been one continual outrage. But you tempt me to speak; I cannot bear to hear the grief in your voice when you speak of life without love. I want you to know that there is one man on earth who worships you; who would come from the ends of the earth to serve you; who will consecrate his days to you, and who will die blessing your name! No, there shall be no time or space for reproaches, for, sweet woman as you are, I know the force of your indignation; I am going away at once, and you need never think of me again. See, I kiss your hands and ask your forgiveness for my roughness, my presumption. I have no right to speak as I have done, I know—but you will have pity—'

He stopped as she gently withdrew her hands from his clasp and gazed at him with sad, wet eyes. There was no anger in her face, only a profound despair.

'Oh, yes, I will have pity,' she murmured vaguely. 'Who would not be pitiful for such a waste of love—of life! It is very cruel and confusing—

one cannot be angry; I grieve for you, and I grieve for myself. You see, in my case, love is now a thing of the past. I have to look back upon it and say with the German poet, "I have lived and loved." I love no more, and therefore I live no more. You, at any rate, have more vitality than I—you are still conscious of love—'

'Bitterly conscious!' said Valdis. 'Hopelessly conscious!'

She was silent for a little; her face was turned away, and Valdis could not see the tears falling from her eyes. Presently she spoke very tranquilly, putting out her hand to meet his.

'My dear friend,' she said, 'I am very sorry! I think you understand my nature, and you will therefore feel instinctively how sorry I am! I am quite an unfortunate mortal; I win love where I never sought it, and I have given love where it is not valued. Let us say no more about it. You are a brave man; you have your work, your art, and your career. You will, I hope, in time forget that Delicia Vaughan ever existed. A few days ago I should certainly have resented the very idea of your loving me as an insult and a slur upon my married life; but when I know that my marriage is a farce—a very devil's mockery of holy union—why! I am not in a position to resent anything! Some women, without being as grief-stricken as I am, or in need of any consolation, hearing such a confession as yours to-night, would fling themselves into your arms and give you love for love; but I cannot do that. I have no love left; and if I had, I would not so forfeit my own self-respect,—or your reverence for me as a woman.'

'Oh, my love, my saint! Forgive me!' cried Valdis, moved by a sudden deep humiliation. 'I should still have kept my secret; I ought never to have spoken!'

She looked at him candidly, the tears still in her eyes and a faint smile trembling on her mouth.

'I am not sure about that,' she said. 'You see, when a woman is very sad and lonely, just as if she had grown suddenly too old and poor to have a friend in the world, there is a wonderful sweetness in the knowledge that someone still loves her, even though she may be quite unable to return that love. That is how I feel to-night; and so I cannot be quite as angry with you as I should like to be!'

She paused, then laid her hand on his arm.

'It is growing dark, Mr. Valdis; will you see me home? My rooms are quite close to the pier, so it will only be a few minutes' walk.'

Silently he turned and walked beside her. Overhead, through slowly-flitting clouds, one or two stars twinkled out for a moment and vanished again, and the solemn measure of the sea around them sounded like the subdued chanting of a dirge.

'Where are you staying?' asked Delicia, presently.

'Nowhere,' he answered quickly. 'I shall go back to town to-night.'

She said nothing further, and they walked slowly off the pier and up a little bit of sloping road, whither Spartan preceded them out of an intelligent desire to show his mistress that though he had only been at Broadstairs a few hours he already knew the house they were staying at. Arrived there, Delicia held out both her hands.

'Good-bye, my dear friend!' she said. 'It is a long good-bye, you know—for it is better you should see as little of me as possible.'

'Is it necessary to make me suffer?' asked Valdis, unsteadily. 'I will obey you in anything; but must you banish me utterly?'

'I do not banish you,' she answered gently. 'I only say I shall honour you more deeply and think you a truer friend than ever, if you will spare yourself and me the pain of constant meeting.'

She looked steadfastly at him; her eyes were grave and sweet; her face pale and tranquil as that of some marble saint in the niche of a votive chapel. His heart beat; all the passion and tenderness of the man were roused. He would have given his life to spare her a moment's grief, and yet this quiet desolation of hers, united to such a holy calm, awed him and kept him mute and helpless. Bending down, he took her hands and raised them reverently to his lips.

'Then good-bye, Delicia!' he said; 'Good-bye, my love—for you will be my love always! God keep you! God bless you!'

Loosening her hands as quickly as he had grasped them, he raised his hat and stood bare-headed in the shadowy evening light, gazing at her as a man might gaze who was looking his last on life itself. Then he turned swiftly and was gone.

For a moment Delicia remained passively watching his retreating figure, her hand on the collar of Spartan, who manifested a wild desire to bound after him and bring him back. Then, shuddering a little, she went into the house and shut herself up alone in her bedroom for an hour. When she came out again her eyes were heavy with the shedding of tears; but such an expression was on her face as might be on the radiant features of an angel. And she was very quiet all that evening, sitting at her window and watching the clouds gradually clear, and the great stars shine out above the sea.

IX

The next day she received her husband's letter, the letter in which he had excused himself altogether and started a complaint against her instead. She glanced over it with a weary sense of disgust, and smiled disdainfully as she thought what a mountain he was trying to make out of the mole-hill of the paragraph in *Honesty*.

'As if any one of the lying tongues of journalism wagging against me could do me such wrong as his open infidelity,' she mused. 'God! How is it that men manage to argue away their own vices as if they were nothing, and yet take every small opportunity they can find for damaging an innocent woman's reputation!'

She flung aside the letter and turned over the morning paper. There she found, under the heading of 'Scene at a London Club,' an account of Aubrey Grovelyn's horse-whipping at the hands of Paul Valdis. The *exposé* of the so-called 'poet,' who, as Mr. Brown, had been steadily booming himself, was cautiously hinted at in darkly ambiguous terms— no journal likes to admit that it has been cleverly fooled by one of its own staff. And great editors, who are anywhere and everywhere except where they should be, namely, in the editorial room, are naturally loth to make public the results of their own inattention to business. They do not like to confess that, in their love of pleasure and their devotion to race-meetings and shooting-parties, it often happens that the very porters guarding the doors of their offices know more about the staff than they do. The porter can tell exactly the hour that Mr. B—— comes in to the office at night, the shortness of the time he stays there, and the precipitate hurry with which he goes home to bed. The porter knows that Mr. B—— is paid five hundred a year for doing hard work at that office during a certain number of hours, and that Mr. B—— seldom looks in for more than one hour, having other work on other papers, about which he says nothing. And that, therefore, Mr. B—— is distinctly 'doing' his editor and proprietor. But as long as editors and proprietors prefer to caper about at the heels of 'swagger' society instead of attending strictly to their duties and to the grave responsibilities of journalism, so long will the British Press be corrupted by underlings, and 'used' for purposes which are neither honourable nor national, nor in any way exact, as reflecting the real current of public opinion. Delicia knew all this of old, hence her indifference to the press generally. She had always been entertained and surprised at the naïve delight with which certain society 'belles' had shown her descriptions of themselves in certain fashionable journals, where their personal attractions were enumerated and discussed as if they were nothing more than cattle in a market. She could never understand what pleasure there was in the vulgar compliments of the cheap paragraphist. And in the same way she never thought it worth while to attach importance to the scurrilities that appeared in similar quarters concerning all those women who stood aloof from self-advertisement and declined to 'give themselves away' by consenting to the maudlin puffery of the 'ladies' paper.' So that the lofty tone of injury her husband assumed in his letter not only struck her as mean, but infinitely grotesque as well. She did not answer him, nor did he write again; and she passed a quiet fortnight at Broadstairs, finishing some literary work she had promised to her publishers at a certain date, and trying to think as little as possible of herself or her private griefs. When she was not engaged in creative composition, she turned to the study of books with almost as much ardour as had possessed her when, at the age of twelve, she had preferred to shut herself up alone and read Shakespeare to any other form of entertainment. And gradually, almost unconsciously to herself, the tone and temper of her mind changed and strengthened; she began to reconcile herself to the idea of the lonely lot which would henceforward be her portion. Turning the matter practically over in her mind, she decided that the best course to adopt would be that of a 'judicial separation.' She would make her husband a suitable 'allowance' (she smiled rather bitterly as she thought what a trouble he would make of it, and how he would fret and fume if he had to do without his four-in-hand and his tandem turn-out), and she herself would travel all over the world and gain fresh knowledge and experience for her literary labours. Or, if constant travel proved to be too fatiguing, she would take some place in the remote Highlands of Scotland, or the beautiful sequestered valleys of Ireland, and make a little hermitage among the hills, where she could devote herself to work and study for the remainder of her days.

'I daresay I shall manage to be at least content, if I am not happy,' she said to herself; 'though, of course, society will reverse the position in its usual eminently false and disgusting way, and will whisper all sorts of lies about me, such as, "Oh, you know a literary woman is impossible to live with! It is always so; poor, dear Carlyon could not possibly stand her, she was so dreadful! Clever, but quite dreadful! Yes, and so they are separated. Such a good thing for Carlyon! He looks ten years younger since he got rid of her! And they say she's living down in the country somewhere not *too* far from town; not *so* far but that Paul Valdis knows where to find her!" Oh, yes, I can hear them all at it,—croaking harpies!' and her small hand clenched involuntarily. 'The vultures of society can never understand anyone loving the sweet savour of truth; they only scent carrion. No man is true in their estimation, no woman pure; and chastity is so far from being pleasing to them that they will not even believe it exists!'

On the last afternoon of her stay at Broadstairs, she spent several hours strolling by the sea, listening to its solemn murmur and watching the sunlight fall in golden lines over its every billow and fleck of foam. With the gravity of her thoughts, her face had grown more serious during the last few days, though it had lost nothing in sweetness of expression; and as she paced along the sand, close to the very fringe of the waves, with Spartan bounding now and then into the water and back with joyous, deep barks of delight, a sudden, inexplicable sense of pain and regret surprised her into tears. Gazing far out beyond the last gleam of the ocean line with longing eyes, she murmured,—

'How strange it is! I feel as if I should never look upon the sea again! I am growing morbid, I suppose, but to my fancy the waves are saying, "Good-bye, Delicia! Good-bye for ever, and still good-bye!" like Tosti's old song!'

She stood silent for a little while, then turned and went homeward, resolutely battling with the curious foreboding that had suddenly oppressed her brain and heart. Spartan, shaking the wet spray from his shaggy coat, trotted by her side in the highest spirits; he was untroubled by any presentiments; he lived for the moment and enjoyed it thoroughly—a habit of mind common to all animals except man.

The next day she returned to London and entered her own house with her usual quiet and unruffled air. She looked well, even happy; and Robson, who opened the door for her admittance, began to think he was wrong after all, and that she 'knew' nothing.

'Is Lord Carlyon in?' she asked, with the civil coldness of a visitor rather than of a wife.

'No, my lady.' Here Robson hesitated, then finally spoke out. 'His lordship has not been home for some days.'

Delicia looked at him steadily, and Robson stammered on, giving her more information.

'Since the grand dinner his lordship gave here last week, he has only called in for his letters; he has been staying with friends.'

Delicia glanced around her at the picturesque hall with its heraldic emblems, stained-glass windows and rare old oak furniture, all of which she had collected herself and arranged with the taste of a perfect artist, and a faint chill crept over her as she thought that perhaps even her home—the home she had built and planned and made beautiful out of the work of her own brain—had been desecrated by the company of her husband's 'private friends.'

'Was it a very grand dinner, Robson?' she asked, forcing a smile, 'Or did you all get into a muddle and do things badly?'

'Well, my lady, we had very little to do with it,' answered Robson, now gaining sufficient courage to pour out his suppressed complaints. 'His lordship ordered all the dinner himself from Benoist, and sent cook and some of the other servants out for the day. They wasn't best pleased about it, my lady. I stayed to help in the waiting. It was a very queer party indeed, but of course it isn't my business to say anything—'

'Go on,' said Delicia, quietly. 'What people dined here? Do I know any of them?'

'Not that I am aware of, my lady,' said Robson, with an injured air. 'I should say it wasn't at all likely you knew any of them; they were very loud in their ways, very loud indeed. Two of the females—I beg pardon—ladies, stayed to sleep—one young one, and one old.'

Trembling from head to foot, Delicia managed still to restrain herself and to speak quietly,—

'Did you know their names?'

'Oh, yes, my lady—Madame de Gascon and her daughter, Miss de Gascon. Their names are French, but they spoke a sort of costermonger's English.'

'Did any of them go into my study?'

'No, my lady,' and honest Robson squared himself proudly. 'I took the liberty of locking the door and putting the key in my pocket, and saying that you had left orders it was to be kept locked, my lady.'

'Thank you!' But as she spoke she quivered with rage and shame— her very servant pitied her; even *he* had had more decency and thought for her than the man she had wedded. Was it possible to drain much deeper the dregs of humiliation?

She went upstairs to her own bedroom and looked nervously about her. Had 'Madame de Gascon and Miss de Gascon,' whoever they were, slept there? She dared not ask; she feared lest she should lose the self control she had practised during her absence, and so be unable to meet her husband with that composure and dignity which her own self-respect taught her would be necessary to maintain. She loosened her cloak and took off her hat, glancing at all the familiar objects around her the while, as though she expected to see them changed. In the evening she would have to go to Lady Dexter's 'crush,' which was being given in her special honour. She determined she would lie down and rest till it was time to dress. But just as she turned towards her bed a sharp pain ran through her body, as though a knife had been plunged into her heart,—a black cloud loomed before her eyes, and she fell forward in a dead swoon. Emily, the maid, who was fortunately in the adjoining dressing-room, heard her fall, and rushed at once to her assistance. With the aid of cold water and smelling-salts, she shudderingly revived and gazed about her in pitiful wonderment.

'Emily, is it you?' she asked feebly. 'What is the matter? Did I faint? What a strange thing for me to do! I remember now; it was a dreadful pain that came at my heart. I thought I was dying—'

She paused, shivering violently.

'Shall I send for the doctor, my lady?' asked the frightened Emily. 'You look very white; you will never be able to go to the party this evening.'

'Oh, yes, I shall,' and with an effort Delicia rose to her feet and tried to control the trembling of her limbs. 'I will sit in this arm-chair and rest, and I shall soon be all right. Go and make me a cup of tea, Emily, and don't say anything about my illness to the other servants.'

Emily, after lingering about a little, left the room at last, with some uneasiness; and when she had gone, Delicia leaned back in her chair and closed her eyes.

'That was a horrible, horrible pain!' she thought. 'I wonder if there is anything wrong with my heart? To-morrow I will see a doctor; to-night I shall want all my strength, physical and moral, to help me to look with calmness on my husband's face.'

Gradually she grew better; her breathing became easier and the nervous trembling of her limbs ceased. When the maid came up with the tea she was almost herself again, and smiled at her attendant's anxious face in a perfectly reassuring manner.

'Don't be frightened, Emily,' she said gently. 'Women often faint, you know; it is nothing extraordinary; it might happen to you any day.'

'Yes, my lady,' stammered Emily. 'But you never have fainted—and—'

'You want me to ask a doctor about myself? So I will to-morrow. But to-night I must look my best.'

'What gown will you wear, my lady?' asked Emily, beginning to regain her wits and composure.

'Oh, the very grandest, of course,' said Delicia, with a little laugh. 'The one with the embroidered train, which you say looks as if it were sewn all over with diamonds.'

Emily's bright face grew more radiant; the care of this special gown was her delight; her mistress had only worn it once, and then had looked such a picture of ethereal loveliness as might have made 'Oberon, the fairy king,' pause in his flight over flowers to wonder at her; and while the willing 'Abigail' busied herself in preparing the adornments of the evening, Delicia sipped her tea and reclined in her chair restfully, thinking all the while strange thoughts that had not occurred to her before.

'If I were to die now,' so ran her musings, 'all the results of my life's work would, by the present tenor of my will, go to my husband. He would care nothing for my fame or honour; his interests would centre round the money only. And with that money he would amuse himself with La Marina or any other new fancy of the hour; possibly my own jewels would be scattered as gifts among his favourites, and I doubt if even my poor, faithful Spartan would find a home for his old age! This must be seen to. I have made a mistake and it must be remedied. Fortunately the law, which is generally so unjust to women, has been forced into permitting our unhappy sex to have at least an individual right over our own money, whether earned or inherited; formerly we were not allowed to have any property apart from our lords and masters! Good heavens! What a heavy score we women shall run up against men at the Day of Judgment!'

The hours wore on, and by the time she was dressed for Lady Dexter's 'at home' she was in one of her most brilliant, vivacious moods. Emily, the maid, stared at her in rapt fascination, as arrayed in the richly-embroidered dress of jewel-work, with its train of soft satin to match, springing from the shoulders and falling in pliant folds to the ground, she stood before her mirror fastening a star of diamonds among her luxuriant hair. Through the rare old lace that fringed the sleeves of her gown, her fair white arms shone like the arms of the marble Psyche; her eyes were dark and luminous, her lips

MARIE CORELLI

red, her cheeks faintly flushed with excitement. A single branch of 'Annunciation' lilies garlanded her dress from waist to bosom, and as she regarded her own fair image she smiled sorrowfully, mentally apostrophising herself thus:—

'No, you are not quite bad-looking, Delicia, but you have one horrible defect—you have got what is called an "expressive" face. That is a mistake! You should not have any expression; it is "bad form" to look interested, surprised, or indignant. A beautiful nullity is what men like—a nullity of face combined with a nullity of brain. You should paint and powder and blacken your eyelashes, and you should also be ready to show your ankles, "by accident," if necessary. The men would find you charming then, Delicia; they would say you had "go" in you; but to be simply a student, with ideas of your own about the world in general, and to write down these ideas in books, which give you a fame and position equal to the fame and position of a man,—this makes you a bore in their eyes, Delicia!—an unmitigated nuisance, and they wish you were well out of their way! If you could only have been a "Living Picture" at the Palace Theatre, or turned out your arms and twiddled your toes in front of the footlights with as few garments on as possible, you would have been voted "clever," Delicia! But being a successful rival with men in the struggle for fame, they vent their spite by calling you a fool. And you are a fool, my dear, to have ever married one of them!'

Smiling at herself disdainfully, she gathered up her fan and gloves, and descended to her carriage. No message had come from Carlyon to say whether or no he meant to be present at the party that evening; but his wife had attained to such an appreciable height of cool self-control, that she now viewed the matter with complete indifference. Arrived at Lord Dexter's stately house in Park Lane, she went to the ladies' room to throw off her wraps, and there found, all alone, and standing well in front of the long mirror, so as to completely block the view for anyone else, a brilliant-looking, painted personage in a pale-green costume, glittering with silver, who glanced up as she entered and surveyed her pearl embroideries with greedy admiration.

'What an awfully sweet gown!' she burst out frankly. 'I always say what I think, though I am told it is rude. It's awfully sweet! I should like just such a one to dance in!'

Delicia looked at her in a haughty silence. The other woman laughed.

'I suppose you think it pretty cool of me making remarks on your clothes,' she said; 'but I'm a "celebrity," you see, and I always say what

I like and do what I like. I'm Violet de Gascon;—*you* know!—the "Marina."'

Frozen into a rigid state of calm, Delicia loosened her lace wrappings with chilly fingers, and allowed the servant in attendance to take them from her.

'Are you?' she then said, slowly and bitterly, 'I congratulate you! As you have given me your name, I may as well give you mine. I am Lady Carlyon.'

'No!' cried 'La Marina,' known in polite society as 'Miss de Gascon,' and to her father in Eastcheap as 'my gal, Jewlia Muggins.' 'No! You don't mean to say you're the famous Delicia Vaughan? Why, I've read all your books, and cried over them, I can tell you! Well now, to think of it!' And her hard, brilliant face was momentarily softened in sudden interest. 'Why, all these swagger people are asked to meet *you* here to-night, and I'm the paid *artiste*. I'm to have forty guineas to dance twice before the assembled company! Tra-la-la!' and she executed a sudden lively pirouette. 'I am pleased! I'd rather dance before you than the Queen!'

In an almost helpless state of amazement, Delicia sat down for a moment and gazed at her. The servant had left the room, and 'La Marina,' glancing cautiously about her, approached on tip-toe, moving with all the silent grace of a beautiful Persian cat. 'I say, she said confidentially, 'you are sweetly pretty! But I suppose you know that; and you're awfully clever, and I suppose you know that too! But why ever did you go and marry such a cad as "Beauty" Carlyon?'

Springing to her feet, Delicia fronted her, her eyes flashing indignation, her breath coming and going, her lips parted to speak, when swift as thought 'La Marina' tapped her fingers lightly against her mouth.

'Don't defend him, you dear thing!' she said frankly. 'He isn't worth it! He thinks he's made a great impression on me, but, lor'! I wouldn't have him as a butler! My heart is as sound as a bell,' and she slapped herself emphatically on the chest, as though in proof of it. 'When I take a lover—a real one, you know,—no sham!—I'll pick out a good, honest, worthy chap from the working classes. I don't care about your "blue blood" coming down from the Conquest, with all the evils of the Conquest fellows in it; it seems to me the older the blood the worse the man!'

Delicia grew desperate. It was no time to play civilities off one against the other; it was a case of woman to woman.

'You know I cannot answer you!' she said hotly. 'You know I cannot speak to you of my husband or myself. Oh, how *dare* you insult me!'

'La Marina' looked at her amazedly with great, wide-open, unabashed black eyes.

'Good gracious!' she exclaimed, 'here's a row! Insult you? I wouldn't insult you for the world; I like your books too much; and now, having seen you, I like *you*. I suppose you've heard your husband runs after me; but, lor'! you shouldn't let that put you out. They all do it—married men most of all. I can't help it! There's the Duke of Stand-Off—he's after me day and night; he's got three children, and his wife's considered a leading beauty. Then there's Lord Pretty-Winks; he went and sold an old picture that's been in his family hundreds of years, and bought me a lot of fal-lals with the proceeds. I didn't want them, and I told him so; but it's all no use—they're noodles, every one of them.'

'But you encourage them,' said Delicia, passionately. 'If you did not—'

'If I did not *pretend* to encourage them,' said 'La Marina,' composedly, 'I should lose all chance of earning a living. No manager would employ me! That's a straight tip, my dear; follow it; it won't lead you wrong!'

But Delicia, with a smarting pain in her eyes and a sense of suffocation in her throat, was forced on by her emotions to put another question.

'Stop—you make me think I have done you an injustice,' she said. 'Do you mean to tell me—that you are—?'

'A good woman?' finished 'La Marina,' smiling curiously. 'No, I don't mean to tell you anything of the sort! I'm not good; it doesn't pay me. But I am not as bad as men would like me to be. Come, let's go into the drawing-room. Or shall I go first? Yes?'—this as Delicia drew back and signed to her to proceed—'All right; you look *sweet*!'

And she swept her green and silver skirts out of the room, leaving Delicia alone to steady her nerves as best she might, and regain her sorely-shaken self-control. And in a few minutes the fashionable crowd assembled at Lady Dexter's stirred and swayed with excitement as all eyes were turned on the sylph-like vision of a fair woman in gleaming white and jewels, with a pale face and dark violet eyes, whose name was announced through the length and breadth of the great drawing-rooms by the servants-in-waiting as 'Lady Carlyon,' but whom all the world of intelligence and culture present whispered of as 'the famous Delicia Vaughan.' For a handle to one's name is a poor thing in comparison to the position of genius; and that the greatest emperor ever crowned is less renowned throughout the nations than plain William Shakespeare, is as it should be, and serves as a witness of the eternal supremacy of truth and justice amid a world of shams.

X

The first person Delicia saw after her hostess on entering the rooms was her husband. She bowed to him serenely, with a charming smile and playful air, as if she had only just left his company, then passed him by, entering at once into conversation with an artist of note, who came eagerly forward to present his young wife to her. Carlyon, quite taken aback, stared at her half-angrily, half-obsequiously, for there was something very queenly in the way she moved, something very noble in the manner she carried her proud little head, on which the diamond star she wore shone like Venus on a frosty night. He watched her slim figure in its white draperies moving hither and thither; he saw the brilliant smile light up her whole countenance and flash in her violet eyes; he watched men of distinction in art and statesmanship crowd about her with courtly flatteries and elegantly-worded compliments, and the more he watched her, the more morose and ill-humoured he became.

'Anyhow,' he muttered to himself, 'she is my wife, and she can't get rid of me. She has no fault whatever to find with me in the eyes of the law!'

He had always been vain of his personality, and it irritated him curiously to notice that she never glanced once in his direction. No one could possibly deny his outward attractiveness—he was distinctly what is called a 'beautiful man.' Beautiful in form and physique, manly in bearing, 'god-like' in feature. Nothing could do away with these facts. And he had imagined that when Delicia—tender, worshipping Delicia—set eyes on him again after her temporary absence from him, her ravishment at the sight of his perfections would be so great that she would fling herself into his arms or at his feet, and, as he expressed it to himself, 'make it all right.' But her aspect this evening was rather discouraging to these hopes, for she seemed not to see him or his attractions at all. She was apparently more fascinated with the appearance of a gouty ambassador, who sat far back in a corner carefully resting one foot on a velvet hassock, and who was evidently afraid to move. To this old gentleman Delicia talked in her most charming manner, and Carlyon, as his eyes wandered about the room, suddenly caught the mischievous and mocking glance of 'La Marina'—a glance which said as plainly as words, 'What a fool you are!' Flushing with annoyance, he moved from the position he had taken up near the grand piano and strolled by himself through the rooms, picking out here and there a few of his own friends to speak to, who, however, seemed to have nothing much to say except, 'How charming Lady Carlyon looks this evening!' a phrase which irritated rather than pleased him, simply because it was true. It was true that Delicia looked lovely; it was true that she eclipsed every woman in the room by her intelligence, grace of manner and brilliancy of conversation; and it was true that for a time at least she was the centre of attraction and absorbed the whole interest of everyone present. And Carlyon was distinctly vexed at the sensation she made, because he had no part in it, because he felt himself left out in the cold, and, moreover, because he was forced to understand that she, his wife, had determined that so he should be left. He would not—perhaps by some defect of brain he could not—realise that he had himself forfeited all claim to her consideration or respect, and he was glad when the arrival of another celebrity was announced, who at once distracted the attention of the frivolous throng from Delicia altogether—a lady of brilliant beauty, and of exalted rank, who had distinguished herself by becoming a *demi-mondaine* of the most open and shameless type, but who, nevertheless, continued to 'move in society,' as the phrase goes, with a considerable amount of *éclat*, simply because she had money, and was wont to assist churches with it and shower pecuniary benefits on penniless clerics. Deity (through the said clerics) blessed her in spite of her moral backslidings; and instead of denouncing her as it should have done, the Church went to her garden-parties. Lady Brancewith was a clever woman in her way, as well as a beautiful one; she loved her own vices dearly, and was prepared to sacrifice anything for the indulgence of them—husband, children, name, fame, honour; but she took a great deal of pains to keep in with 'pious' people, and she knew that the best way to do that was continually to give *largesse* all round. The worthy clergyman of the parish in which her great house was the chiefest of the neighbourhood, shut his eyes to her sins and opened them to her cheques; so all went well and merrily with her. Her entrance into Lady Dexter's drawing-room was the signal for a complete change in the attitude of the fashionable throng. Everybody craned their necks to look at her and comment on her dress and diamonds; people began to whisper to each other the newest bits of scandal about her, and Delicia, with her fair face and unsullied character, was soon deserted and forgotten. She was rather glad of this, and she sat down in a retired corner to rest, near the entrance to the great conservatory, where the curtains shaded her from the light, and where she could see without being seen. She watched the smiles and gestures of Lady Brancewith with a good deal of inward pain and contempt.

'That is the kind of "society woman" men like,' she mused, 'One who will go down into the mud with them and never regret the loss of cleanliness. I think she is a worse type than "La Marina," for "La Marina" does not pretend to be good; but this woman's whole life is occupied in the despicable art of feigning virtue.'

She remained in her quiet nook looking at the restless, talking, giggling throng, and now and then turning her eyes towards the flowers in the conservatory—tall lilies, brilliant azaleas, snowy Cape jessamine, drooping passion flowers—all exquisite creations of perfect beauty, yet silent and seemingly unconscious of their own charms.

'How much more lovely and worthy of love flowers are than human beings!' she thought. 'If I had been the Creator, I think I would have given the flowers immortal souls, rather than to men!'

At that moment her husband passed her without perceiving her. Lady Brancewith was on his arm, evidently delighted to be seen in the company of so physically handsome a person. The little diamonds sewn on her priceless lace flashed in Delicia's eyes like sparks of light; the faint, sickly odour of patchouli was wafted from her garments as she moved; the hard lines which vice and self-indulgence had drawn on that fair face were scarcely perceptible in the softened light, and her little low laugh of coquettish pleasure at some remark of Lord Carlyon's sounded musical enough even to Delicia, who, though she knew and detested the woman's character, could not refrain from looking after her half in wonderment, half in aversion. Within a few paces of where she sat they stopped,—Lord Carlyon placed a chair for his fair companion near a giant palm, which towered up nearly to the roof of the conservatory, and then, drawing another to her side, sat down himself.

'At last in my wretched life I am allowed a moment's pleasure!' he said, conveying into his fine eyes a touch of the Beautiful Sullenness expression which he generally found answer so well with women.

Lady Brancewith laughed, unfurling her fan.

'Dear me, how very tragic!' she said. 'I had, no idea you were so wretched, Lord Carlyon! On the contrary, I thought you were one of the most envied of men!'

Carlyon was silent a moment, looking at her intently.

'The only man in the world to be really envied is your husband,' he said morosely.

Delicia, hidden by the protecting curtain, kept herself quite still. A smile of disdain came on her proud mouth as she thought within herself, 'What liars men are! I have heard him say often that Lord Brancewith ought to be hounded out of the clubs for allowing his wife to dishonour his name! And now he declares him to be the only man in the world to be really envied!'

But Carlyon was speaking again, and some force stronger than herself held her there motionless, an unwilling listener.

'You have never been kind to me,' he complained, the Beautiful Sullenness look deepening in his eyes. 'Lots of other fellows get a chance to make themselves agreeable to you, but you never give me the ghost of one. You are awfully hard on me—Lily!'

He paused a moment before uttering Lady Brancewith's Christian name, then spoke it softly and lingeringly, as though it were a caress. She, by way of reply, gave him a light tap on the cheek with her fan.

'And you are awfully impertinent,' she said, smiling. 'Don't you remember you are a married man?'

'I do, to my cost,' he answered. 'And you are a married woman!'

'Oh, but I am so different,' she declared naïvely. 'You see, you have got a wonderful celebrity for a wife—clever and brilliant, and all that. Now, poor Brancewith is a dreadful, dear old dunce, and I should really die if I hadn't some other man to speak to sometimes—'

'Or several other men!' he put in, taking her fan from her hand and beginning to wave it to and fro.

She laughed.

'Perhaps! How jealous you are! Do you treat your wife to these sort of sarcasms?'

'I wish you wouldn't talk about my wife,' he said pettishly. 'My wife and I have nothing in common.'

'Really!' Lily Brancewith yawned slightly. 'How often that happens in married life, doesn't it? She is here to-night, isn't she?'

'Yes, she is in the rooms somewhere,' and Carlyon began to look decidedly cross. 'She was quite the centre of attraction till you came in. Then, of course, it was a case of a small star paling before the full moon in all her splendour!'

'How sweetly poetical! But please don't break my fan,' and she took the delicate toy in question from him. 'It cost twenty guineas, and it isn't paid for yet.'

'Let me settle the bill,' said Carlyon, looking adoringly into her eyes, 'or any amount of bills!'

A faint tremor ran through Delicia's body, as though a cold wind were playing on her nerves. Bending a little forward, she listened more intently.

'Generous man!' laughed Lady Brancewith. 'I know your wife has made you rich, but I remember the time when you were not a bit flush of money, were you, poor boy! But you were always very nice and very complimentary, even then.'

'Glad you admit it,' said Carlyon, drawing a little nearer to her. 'The memory of it may decide you not to throw me over now!'

'What nonsense you talk!' and Lady Brancewith gave him her hand to hold. 'I want to see your wife; do introduce me to her! I have often been on the point of meeting her, but never have done so. *She* doesn't know the people I know, and *I* don't know the people she knows, so we've always missed each other. She is such a genius! Dunce as you are, you must have sense enough to be very proud of her!'

Carlyon looked dubious. Then he suddenly said,—

'Well, I don't know! I think a clever woman—a writer of books, you know, like my wife—is a mistake. She is always *unsexed*.'

As the word passed his lips, Delicia rose, pale, fair and calm in her glistening robes, and confronted them. Like an austere white angel suddenly descended from heaven to earth she stood,—quite silent,—looking straight at her husband and his companion with such a grand scorn in her dark violet eyes as made Carlyon shrink within himself like a beaten hound. Lady Brancewith glanced up at her with a half-impertinent, half-questioning smile, but not a word did Delicia utter. One moment she stood surveying the disloyal, ungracious and ungrateful churl who owed all he possessed in the world to her tenderness and bounty; then coldly, quietly, and with an unshaken grace of bearing and queenliness of movement, she turned away, her soft satin train sweeping them by as she moved forward into the crowded rooms and disappeared.

'Who was that wonderful-looking woman?' asked Lady Brancewith, eagerly.

Carlyon flushed, anon grew deadly pale.

'That was Delicia—my wife,' he answered curtly.

'That! That the novelist!' almost screamed Lady Brancewith. 'Why didn't you say so? Why didn't you introduce me? I had no idea she was like that! I thought all literary women wore short hair and spectacles! Good gracious me! And she must have heard you say you considered her "unsexed!" Billy, what a brute you are!'

Carlyon started angrily. The fair Lily and he used in former days to call each other 'Billy' and 'Lily' so frequently that a wag among their acquaintance made a rhyme on them, running thus:—

> 'Lily and Billy
> Are invariably silly!

and at that time he did not mind it. But now, considering that he was 'Lord' Carlyon, he did not care to be addressed as 'Billy,' and his resentment showed itself pretty plainly on his darkened countenance. But Lady Brancewith was too much excited to heed his annoyance.

'The idea!' she continued. 'If she was sitting there all the while she must have heard *everything*! A nice mess you have made of it! If I were in her place, I'd throw you off like a pair of old shoes!'

'I haven't the least doubt you would,' he said with temper. 'It's the way you behave with most men who have the honour of sharing your favour!'

Lily Brancewith showed her pearly teeth in a savage little smile.

'You were always what is called "rather shady," Billy,' she observed calmly. 'But I didn't give you credit for being *quite* a cad! Ta-ta! I'm going to find your wife and introduce myself to her. You know in society people said you were to be pitied for marrying a "literary" celebrity, but I shall put the gossips right on that point—I shall tell everybody it is she who is to be pitied for marrying a military nonentity!'

With a light laugh at her own sarcasm she left him, and started on a voyage of discovery after Delicia. The people were wedged together in groups at every available point to watch the dancing of "La Marina," who had commenced her performance, and who was announced for that evening as 'Mademoiselle Violet de Gascon' out of deference to the 'proprieties,' who might possibly have been shocked had they been too openly told that the *figurante* was the 'Empire's' famous 'Marina,' though they were quite aware of the fact all the time. For in the strange motley we call society, one of the chief rules is that if you know a truth you must never say it; you must say something else, as near to a lie as possible. For example, if you are aware, and everybody else is aware, that a lady of exalted title has outraged, or is outraging, every sense of decency and order in her social and private life, you must always say she is one of the purest and most innocent creatures living. *Of* course, if she is a nobody, without any rank at all, you are at liberty to give her poor name over to the dogs of slander to rend at will; but if she is a countess or a duchess, you must entirely condone her vulgar vices. Think of her title! Think of her family connections! Think of the manner in which her influence might be brought to bear on some little matter in which you personally have an interest! Lady Brancewith knew all this well enough; she knew exactly how to play her cards, and she was sufficiently a woman of the world to salute 'La Marina' with a pretty bow and compliment as soon as her dance was finished, and to express the plaintive wish, uttered sighingly, 'How glad I should be if I were half so clever!'

Whereat Marina sniffed the air dubiously and said nothing. 'Jewlia Muggins,' *alias* 'Violet de Gascon,' knew a thing or two, and was not to be taken in by Lady Brancewith or any of her set. She was keenly disappointed. Delicia had not been present to see her dance, and she had very much wished to create a favourable impression on that 'sweet thing in white' as she called her. She had danced her best, gracefully, and with an exquisite modesty; too exquisite for many of the gentlemen assembled, some of whom whispered to each other that she was 'going off' a bit, simply because they could not see much above her slender ankles. She herself, however, cared nothing for what they said or thought, and at the conclusion of her dance she boldly asked her hostess where Lady Carlyon was.

'She has gone home, I am sorry to say,' was the reply. 'She is not very well, she tells me; and she found the heat of the room rather trying.'

'Are you speaking of the guest of the evening—Lady Carlyon?' inquired Lady Brancewith, sweetly.

'Yes. She extremely regretted having to leave so early, but she works hard, you know, and she is not at all robust.'

Here Lady Dexter's attention was distracted by the claims of a long-haired violinist desirous of performing a 'classical' piece immediately, which, when it did begin, had the effect of driving many people down to supper or out of the house altogether; and in the general scrimmage on the stairs 'La Marina' found herself elbowing Lord Carlyon.

'Your wife's gone home,' she said curtly. 'Why didn't you go with her?'

'I have another engagement,' he answered coldly.

'Not with me!' she said, showing all her even white teeth in a broad grin. 'I talked ever so long to Lady Carlyon this evening, and told her just what I thought of you!'

His eyes darkened furiously, and the lines of his mouth grew hard and vindictive.

'You wild cat!' he said savagely. 'If you have *dared*—'

'Puss, puss! Pretty puss!' laughed Marina. 'Cats have claws, my Lord Bill, and they scratch occasionally!'

With a swish of her silken skirts she darted past him into the supper-room, where she immediately became surrounded by a circle of young noodles, who evidently deemed it a peculiar glory and honour to be allowed to hand chicken salad to the gifted creature who nightly knocked her own nose with her foot in the presence of a crowded house. What was any art compared to this? What was science? What was learning? What was virtue? Nothing,—less than nothing! To have a shapely leg and know how to hit your nose with your foot, is every day proved to be the best way for a woman to have what is called a 'good time' in this world. She needn't be able to spell, she may drop her h's broadcast, she may 'booze' on brandy,—but so long as the nose is hit every night with the foot in an accurate and rhythmic manner, she will always have plenty of jewels and more male admirers than she can conveniently manage. For there is no degradation that can befall a woman which man will not excuse and condone; equally there is no elevation or honour she can win which he will not grudge and oppose with all the force of his nature! For man loves to hold a strangulation-grip on the neck of all creation, women included; and the idea that woman should suddenly wrench herself out of his grasp and refuse to be either trapped like a hare, hunted like a fox, or shot like a bird, is a strange, new and disagreeable experience for him. And very naturally he clings to the slave type of womanhood, and encourages the breed of those who are willing to become dancers and toys of his 'harem,' for, if all women were to rise to the height of their true and capable dignity, where should he go to for his so-called 'fun'?

Some thoughts of this kind were in Lord Carlyon's head as he threw on his opera-coat and prepared to leave the scene of revelry at the Dexters. The pale, noble face of Delicia haunted him; the disdain of her clear eyes still rankled in his soul; and he was actually indignant with her for what he considered 'that offensive virtue of hers,' which

MARIE CORELLI

shamed him, and which had, for a moment at least, made 'the most distinguished Lady Brancewith' seem nothing but a common drab, daubed with paint and powder. Even as he thought of her thus, the fair and faithless Lily approached him, smiling, with a coaxing and penitent air.

'Still huffy?' she inquired sweetly. 'Poor, dear thing! Did it fret and fume and turn nasty?' She laughed, then added, 'Don't be cross, Billy! I was very rude to you just now—I'm sorry! See!' and she folded her hands with an appealing air. 'Drive home with me, will you? I'm so lonely! Brancewith's at Newmarket.'

Carlyon hesitated, looking at her. She was undoubtedly very lovely, despite her artificial flesh tints and distinctly dyed hair.

'All right!' he said with a stand-offish manner of coldness and indifference, 'I don't mind seeing you home.'

'How sweet and condescending of you!' and Lady Brancewith threw on her mantle gleaming with iridescent jewels and showered with perfumed lace. 'So good of you to bore yourself with my company!'

Her eyes flashed; she was in a dangerous mood, and Carlyon saw it. In silence he piloted her through the ranks of attendant flunkeys, and when her carriage came bowling up to the door assisted her into it.

'Good-night!' he then said, raising his hat ceremoniously.

Lily Brancewith turned white with sudden passion.

'Aren't you coming in?' she asked.

He smiled, thoroughly enjoying the position.

'No, I have changed my mind. I am going home—to my wife!'

Lady Brancewith trembled, but quickly controlled herself.

'So right of you,' she said, smiling. 'So proper!' Then, putting out her hand, she caught him by the coat-sleeve. 'Do you know what I wish for you?' she said slowly.

'Can't imagine!' he responded carelessly. 'Something nasty, no doubt.'

'Yes, it is something nasty!' She laughed under her breath as she spoke. 'Something nasty, yet very commonplace, too. I wish your wife may discover the kind of man you are,—and *stop your allowances*! Good-night!'

She smiled brilliantly; the horses started suddenly and he drew back, smothering an angry oath. Another moment and the carriage had rolled away, leaving him alone staring at the pavement. He stood for a little lost in gloomy meditation; then, summoning a hansom, was driven home at a brisk pace, having made up his mind to 'face it out,' as he inwardly said, with Delicia.

'She can't help loving me,' he mused. 'She always has loved me, and she is not a woman likely to change her feelings in a hurry. I'm sorry she saw me with Lily Brancewith; and of course, if that jade Marina has really been talking to her there'll be a devil of a row. I must make it right with her somehow, and I think I know the best way to go to work.' Here he smiled. 'Poor little woman! I daresay she feels awfully sore; but I know her character—a few loving words and plenty of kisses and embraces, and she'll be just the same as ever she was, and—and—by Jove! I'll see if I can't turn over a new leaf. It'll be infernally dull, but I'll try it!'

And perfectly satisfied with the plan he had formulated in his own mind for setting things straight, he arrived at his own house. The door was opened to him by Robson, who informed him that her ladyship had returned about an hour ago and was waiting to see him in her study.

'In her study, did you say?' he repeated.

'Yes, my lord. Her ladyship said, would you kindly go up at once, as soon as you came in.'

A touch of 'nerves' affected him as he threw off his coat and began to ascend the stairs. He saw Robson extinguish the gas in the hall and descend kitchenwards, and a great silence and darkness seemed to encompass the house as he paused for a moment outside his wife's room. Then, slowly and with some hesitation, he lifted the velvet *portière* and entered.

XI

Delicia was at her desk, writing. She had taken off her rich evening costume and was clad in a loose robe of white cashmere that fell down to her feet, draping her after the fashion of one of Fra Angelico's angels. Her hair was unbound from its 'dress coiffure' of elaborate twists and coils, and was merely thrust out of her way at the back of her head in one great knot of gold. She rose as her husband entered, and turned her face, deadly pale and rigid as a statue's, full upon him. He paused, looking at her, and felt his braggart courage oozing out at his fingers' ends.

'Delicia,' he began, making a poor attempt at smiling. 'Delicia, I am awfully sorry—'

Her eyes, full of a burning indignation, flashed upon him like lightning and struck him, despite himself, into silence.

'Spare yourself and me any further lies!' she said, in a low voice that vibrated with intense passion. 'There is no longer any need of them. You have shown me yourself as you are, in your true colours—the mask has fallen, and you need not stoop to pick it up and put it on again. It is mere waste of time!'

He stared at her, foolishly pulling at his moustache and still trying to smile.

'You called me "unsexed" to-night,' she went on, never removing her steadfast gaze from his face. 'Do you know what the word means? If not, I will tell you. It is to be like the women you admire!—to be like "La Marina," who strips her body to the gaze of the public without either shame or regret; it is to be like Lady Brancewith, who flings her husband's name and honour to the winds for any fool to mock at, and who in her high position is worse, yes, worse than "La Marina," who at any rate is honest in so far that she admits her position and makes no pretence of being what she is not! But I,—what have *I* done that you should call me "unsexed?"'

She paused, breathing quickly.

'I didn't say *you* were "unsexed," he stammered awkwardly. 'I said clever women were, as a rule, unsexed.'

'Pardon me,' she interrupted him coldly. 'You said "women who write books, like my wife." Those were your exact words. And, I repeat, what have I done to deserve them? Have I ever dishonoured your name? Have you not been the one thought, the one pride, the one love of my life? Has not every beat of my heart, together with every stroke of my pen, been for you and you only? While all the time to me you have played traitor—your very looks have been lies, you have deceived and destroyed all my most sacred beliefs and hopes; you have murdered me as thoroughly as if you had thrust a knife through my heart and hurled me down dead at your feet!'

Her voice vibrated with passion—strong, deeply-felt passion, unshaken by the weakness of sobs or tears.

He made a step towards her.

'Look here, Delicia,' he said, 'don't let us have a scene! I have been a fool, I daresay—I am quite willing to admit it—but can't you forget and forgive?' And undeterred by the chill aversion in her face, he held out his arms. 'Come, I am sure your own heart cannot tell you to be unkind to me! You do love me—'

'Love you!' she cried, recoiling from him; 'I hate you! Your very presence is hideous to my sight; and just as I once thought you the noblest of men, so I think you now the lowest, the meanest! You have been a fool, you say; oh, if you were only that! Only a fool! There are so many of them! Some of them such good fellows, too, in their folly. Fools there are in plenty who, nevertheless, do manage to preserve some cleanliness in their lives; who would not wrong a woman or insult her for the world—fools whom, mayhap, it might be good to love and to work for, and who at any rate are not cads or cowards!'

He started, and the colour leapt to his face in a shamed red, then died away, leaving him very pale.

'Oh, if you are going to rant and scream—' he began.

She turned upon him with a regal air.

'Lord Carlyon, to rant and scream is not my *métier*,' she said. 'I leave that to the poor "Marina," when you have dosed her with too much champagne. There is no need to go over the cause of our present conflict; what I have to say can be said in very few words. Your "unsexed" wife, who has had the honour of maintaining you ever since your union with her, by the ungrudging labour of her brain and hand, has sufficient sense of justice and self-respect to continue no longer in that eminently unpractical mode of action. We must for the future live apart; for I cannot consent to share your attentions with one stage *artiste* or any number of stage *artistes*. I do not choose to pay for their jewels; and your generous offer to settle Lady Brancewith's bills for her does not meet with my consent or approval.

Her face grew colder and more contemptuous as she continued,—

'Your estimate of what is called a "clever" woman is as low as that of most men. I do not especially blame you for being like the rest of your sex in that one particular. Women who will not become as dirt under a man's foot, to be trodden on first, then kicked aside, are generally termed "unsexed," because they will not lower themselves to the man's brute level. Nothing is more unnatural from a man's point of view than that a woman should have brains,—and with those brains make money and position often superior to his, and at any rate manage to be independent of him. What men prefer is that their wives should be the slaves of their humour, and receive a five-pound note with deep thankfulness whenever they can get it, shutting their eyes to the fact that people like "Marina" get twenty pounds to their five from the same quarter. But you,—you have had nothing to complain of in the way of a pecuniary position, though I, as bread-winner, might readily have comported myself after approved masculine examples and given you five pounds where I spent twenty on myself and my own pleasure. But I did nothing of this sort; on the contrary, I have trusted you with half of everything I earned, believing you to be honest; believing that, of all men in the world, you would never cheat, defraud, or otherwise deceive me. And not only have you made a mock of me in society, but you have even helped to vilify my name. For it was distinctly your business to chastise the writer of that lying paragraph in the paper; but you left me to be defended by one who shares with me the drawback of being a "public character," and with whom I have no connection whatever beyond that of friendship, as you perfectly well know. Why, I have heard of men, well-born, too, and of considerable social attainment, who have been willing enough to fight for the so-called "honour" of an admitted *demi-mondaine*; but for an honest woman and faithful wife, who is there in these days that will stir a finger to defend her from slander! Very few; least of all her husband! To such a height has nineteenth-century morality risen! I, who have been true to you in every thought, word and deed, am rewarded by your open infidelity, and for my work, which has at any rate kept you in ease and comfort, I am called "unsexed," despite my pains! If I chose, I could fling you back your insult; for a man who lives on a woman's earnings is more "unsexed" than the woman who earns. I never thought of this before; my love was too blind, too passionate. Now I do think of it; and thinking, I wonder at myself and you!'

He dropped lazily into a chair and looked at her.

'I suppose your temper will be over presently,' he said, 'and you will see things in a more reasonable light. You must remember I have given you a great position, Delicia; I think our marriage has been one of perfect mutual benefit. "Literary" women hardly ever get a chance of marrying at all, you know; men are afraid of them—won't marry them on any account;—would rather have a barmaid, really—and when a "literary" woman gets into the aristocracy and all that—well, by Jove!—it's a splendid thing for her, you know, and gives her a great lift! As for being unfaithful to you, why, there is not a man in my "set" who is absolutely immaculate; I am no worse than any of them—in fact, I am much better. You read so much, and you write so much, that you ought to know these things without my telling them to you. "Give and take" is the only possible rule in marriage, and I really thought you would have good sense enough to admit it—'

Delicia regarded him with a chill smile.

'I think I *have* admitted it!' she said ironically. 'Fully and freely! For I have given everything; equally you have taken everything! That is plain enough. And now you insult me afresh by the suggestion that it was really a condescension on your part to marry me at all, I being "literary"! If I had been a music-hall dancer, of course you would have been much prouder of me; it would have been something indeed worth boasting of, to say your wife had originally been famous for a break-down or can-can at the "Empire!" But because I follow, with what force and ability I can, the steps of the truly great, who have helped to mould the thoughts and feelings of men and nations, it is quite extraordinary I should have found a husband at all! Wonderful! And you have given me a great position, you assert. I confess I fail to perceive it! If you consider your title something of value, I am sorry for you; to me it is a nothing. In the old days of chivalry titles meant honour; now they have become, for the most part, the mere results of wealth and back-stair influence. Yours is an old title, I grant you that; but what does it matter? The latest brewer raised to the peerage puts himself on an equality with you, whether you like it or not. But between me—untitled Delicia Vaughan—and the self-same peer of the ale-cask, there is a great gulf fixed; and not all his wealth can put him on an equality with *me*, or with any author who has once won the love of nations. And so, Lord Carlyon, permit me to return your title, for I shall not wear it. When we separate I shall keep to my own name simply; thus I shall owe you nothing, not even *prestige*!'

Carlyon suddenly lifted his fine eyes and flashed them effectively at her.

'You are talking nonsense, Delicia,' he said impatiently. 'You know you don't really mean that we are to separate. Why,' this with the most naïve conceit, 'what will you do without me?'

She met his gaze without the least emotion.

'I shall continue to live, I suppose,' she replied, 'or I shall die, one of the two. It really doesn't matter which.'

There was a slight tremor in her voice, and emboldened by it he sprang up and tried to put his arm round her. She recoiled from him swiftly, thrusting him back.

'Don't touch me,' she cried wildly. 'Don't dare to come near me! I cannot answer for myself if you do; this shall defend me from you if necessary!'

And almost before he could realise it she had snatched a small, silver-mounted pistol from its case on a shelf hard by, and, holding it in her hand, she stood as it were at bay.

He gave a short, embarrassed laugh.

'You have gone mad, Delicia!' he said. 'Put down that thing. It isn't loaded, of course; but it doesn't look pretty to see you with it.'

'No, it doesn't look pretty,' she responded slowly. 'But it *is* loaded! I took care of that before you came in! I don't want to injure either you or myself; but I swear to you that if you come closer to me by one step, presume to offer me such an insult as your caress would be to me *now*, I will kill you!'

Her white figure was firm as that of some menacing fate carved in marble; her pale face, with the violet eyes set in it like flashing stars, had a marvellous power and passion imprinted on its every line, and despite himself he fell back startled and in a manner appalled.

'I have gone mad, you think?' she went on. 'If I had, would it be wonderful? To have one's dearest hopes ruined, one's heart broken, one's life made waste—is that not something of a cause for madness? But I am not mad; I am simply resolved that your lips, which have bestowed their kisses on "la Marina," shall never touch mine again; that your arms, which have embraced her, shall never embrace me, and that, come what will, I will keep my self-respect if I die for it! Now you know my mind, you will go your way; I mine. I cannot divorce you; for though you have murdered my very soul in me, brutally and pitilessly, you have not been "cruel" according to legal opinion. But I can separate from you—thank God for that! I cannot marry again. Heaven forbid that I should ever desire to do so! Neither can you; but you will not wish for that unless you meet with an American heiress with several millions, which you may have the chance of doing when I am dead—someone who has inherited her money and has not *worked* for it as I have,—honestly,—thereby becoming "unsexed!"'

He stood silent for a minute.

'You actually mean to say you want a judicial separation?' he inquired at last, sullenly.

She bent her head in the affirmative.

'Well, you can get that, of course. But I must say, Delicia, of all the ungrateful, heartless women, you are the very worst! I should never have thought it of you! I imagined you had such a noble nature! So sweet and loving and forgiving! Good heavens! After all, what have I done? Just had a bit of fun with a dancing girl! Quite a common amusement with men of my class!'

'I have no doubt of it,' she answered; 'Very common! All the same, I do not choose to either tolerate it or pay for it. Ungrateful, heartless "unsexed"! This is my character, according to your estimate of me. I thank you! Poor Love's last breath went in that final blow from the rough fist of ingratitude! I will not detain you any longer; in truth, you need not have stayed so long. I merely wished to let you know my decision. I had no intention to either upbraid you or condemn. Reproaches or complaints, however just, could leave no impression on a temperament like yours. I will see my lawyers to-morrow, and in a very short space of time you will be free of my company for ever. Shall we say good-bye now?'

She raised her eyes,—her gold hair shone about her like an aureole, and a sudden sweetness softened her face, though its gravity was unchanged. A sharp pang of remorse and sorrow stabbed him through and through, and he looked at her in mingled abasement and yearning.

'Delicia—must we part?'

He whispered the question, half in hope half in fear.

She regarded him steadily.

'Dare you ask it? Can you imagine I could love you again after what has passed? Some women might do so—I could not.'

He stood irresolute; there was a mean and selfish trouble at his heart to which he could not give utterance for very shame's sake. He was really wondering what arrangements she meant to make for his future, but some few of the better instincts of manhood rose up within him protestingly, and bade him hold his peace. Still the brooding egotistical thought lingered in him and made him angry; he grew more and more wrathful as he realised that she,—this woman, whose whole life and devotion he had had so recently in his keeping,—had suddenly fathomed his true nature and cast him from her as something contemptible, and that she—she had the power to maintain herself free of him in wealth and ease, whilst he, if she were at all malevolently inclined, would have to return to the state of semi-poverty and 'living on tick,' which had been his daily and yearly lot before he met her. Inwardly he cursed 'la Marina,' Lily Brancewith and everybody, except himself. He never thought of including his own vices in the general big 'Damn!' he was mentally uttering. And as he hesitated, shuffling one foot against the other, a prey to the most disagreeable reflections, Delicia advanced a step and held out her hands.

'Good-bye, Will! I loved you once very deeply; a few days ago you were everything to me, and for the sake of that love, which has so suddenly perished and is dead for ever, let us part in peace!'

But he turned from her roughly.

'Oh, it is all very well for you!' he said. 'You can afford to talk all this high-falutin' rubbish, and give yourself airs and graces, but I am a poor devil of a fellow always getting into a hole; and it isn't to be supposed that I am going to take my dismissal in this way, just as if I were a lackey. I am your husband, you know; you can't undo that!'

'Not at present,' said Delicia, drawing back from him quickly, the tenderness passing from her face and leaving it coldly disdainful. 'But it is very possible the Gordian knot of marriage may be cut for me sooner or later. Death may befriend me in this matter, if nothing else will.'

'Death! Nonsense! I am not likely to die, nor are you. And I don't see what you want to get a separation for. I will go away for a time if you like. I will make any promises you want me to make; but why you should bring a lawyer into it, I cannot imagine. The fact is, you are making a fuss about nothing, and I am not going to say good-bye at all. I will take a trip abroad, and by the time I come back I daresay all this will have blown over and you will be glad to see me.'

She said nothing, but simply turned from him, and sitting quietly down at her desk resumed the letter she had been writing when he entered.

'Do you hear me?' he repeated querulously. 'I sha'n't say good-bye.'

She did not speak; her pen moved swiftly over the paper before her, but otherwise she never moved.

'I am sure it is no wonder,' he continued crossly, 'that the Government protests against too much independence being allowed to women! What tyrants they would all become if they could have everything their own way as much as you can! Women ought to be gentle and submissive; and if they are fortunate enough to be wealthy, they ought to use their wealth for their husbands' benefit. That is the natural order of creation—woman was made to be subservient to man, and when she is not, things always go wrong.'

Still Delicia wrote on without uttering a word.

He paused a moment, then observed,—

'Well, I'm quite worn out with all this rumpus! I shall go to bed. Good-night, Delicia!'

At this she turned and looked at him fully.

'Good-night!' she said.

Something in the transparent beauty of her face and the dark tragedy of her eyes awed him. She looked as if during the past few minutes she had risen above and beyond him to a purer atmosphere than that of earth. The majority of men hate women who look so; and Carlyon was painfully conscious that he had suddenly grown to hate Delicia. She had entirely changed, he thought. From a loving, tender idolater of his manly graces and perfections, she had become a proud, cynical, fault-finding, unforgiving 'virago.' This latter term did not suit her at all, but he considered that it did; for, as usual, by the aid of man's logic, he deemed himself the injured party and she the injuring. And irritated beyond measure at the queenly tranquillity of her demeanour, he muttered something profane under his breath, and dashing aside the *portière* with a clatter of its brazen rings and a violence that threatened to tear its very substance, he left the room.

As soon as he had gone, Delicia moved slowly to the door and shut and locked it after him; then as slowly returned to her chair, where, leaning her head back against the carved escutcheon, she quietly fainted.

XII

Next day Delicia was too weak and broken in body and spirit to leave her bedroom, which she had managed to reach by herself on recovering from her swoon. Her husband sent her a brief note of farewell by one of the servants. He was leaving London immediately for Paris, he said, 'and when all this nonsense had blown over,' he would return. Till then he was 'hers affectionately.' She crumpled the note in her hand and lay still, her fair head fallen wearily back among her pillows, and a great sense of exhaustion and fatigue numbing all her faculties. A batch of letters came by the mid-day post, letters from strangers and friends, all warmly testifying as usual to her genius; and as she read she sighed heavily and wondered what was the use of it all?

'They do not know I am dead!' she said to herself, 'That all my life is done with—finished! If I had never known the meaning of love; if I had never thought and believed that love was truly mine, how much better it would have been for me! I should have worked on contentedly; I should not have missed what I had no experience of, and I might—yes, I might have been really great. Now there is no hope for any more attainment—Love has murdered me!'

She rested in bed all day, dozing and dreaming and thinking; all night between the slow-pacing hours she had long waking intervals of strange, half-troubled, half-mystic musings. She saw herself, so she imagined, dead;—laid out in her coffin with flowers round her; but as she looked at her own stiffened corpse she knew it was not herself, she thus saw, but only the image of what she had been. She, Delicia, was another being—a being through whose fine essence light and joy were flowing. She fancied she heard sweet voices murmuring in her ears,—

'Sorrowful Delicia! Slain Delicia! This is not thine end—work has but begun for thee, though earth has no more part in either thy toil or pleasure! Come, Delicia! Love is not dead because of human treachery; Love is immortal, unconquerable, unchangeable, and waits for thee elsewhere, Delicia! Come and see!'

And so persistently was she haunted by the impression that something new and strange awaited her, that almost unconsciously to herself she began to be expectant of a sudden change in her destinies, though what that change might be she could not by herself determine.

When she rose from her bed to resume her daily work an idea flashed upon her,—an idea bold and new, and suggesting itself forcibly for brief and brilliant literary treatment. Seized by this fresh inspiration, she shut herself up in her study and worked day after day, forgetting her own troubles in the fervour of creative energy. She saw no visitors and went nowhere; her morning ride was all the relaxation she permitted herself; and she grew paler and paler as she toiled unremittingly with her pen, and lived a life of almost unbroken solitude all through the height of the London 'season.' The people one calls by courtesy 'friends,' grew tired of leaving cards which were not responded to, and 'society' began to whisper that 'it was rather singular, my dear, that Lord Carlyon should suddenly have left London and gone by himself to Paris, while that extremely peculiar wife of his remained at home shut up as closely as if she had the small-pox.' 'Perhaps she *had* the small-pox,' suggested the Noodle section of opinion, deeming the remark witty. Whereupon Lady Brancewith, joining in the general chitter-chatter, ventured upon the scathing observation that 'if she had, it would make her more popular in society, as no one could then be angry with her for her good looks.' Which suggestion was voted 'charming' of Lady Brancewith; and 'so generous of Lady Brancewith, being so lovely herself, to even consider for a moment in a favourable light the looks of a "female authoress!"— quite too sweet of Lady Brancewith!'

And the inane whispering of such tongues as wag without any brains to guide them went on and on, and Delicia never heard them. Her old friends, the Cavendishes, had left London for Scotland—they hated the 'season' with all the monotony of its joyless round—so that there was no one in town whom she particularly cared to see, And, like the enchanted 'Lady of Shalott,' she sat in her own small study weaving her web of thought, or, as her husband had once put it, 'spinning cocoons.'

Only on one special day was there a break in her self-imposed routine. This occurred when two elderly gentlemen of business-like demeanour arrived carrying small black bags. They were lawyers, and were shown up to the famous author's study at once, where they remained in private converse with her for the greater part of the afternoon.

When they came down again to the dining-room, where wine and biscuits were prepared for their refreshment, Delicia accompanied them; her face was very pale, yet calm, and she had the look of one whose mind has been relieved of an oppressive burden.

MARIE CORELLI

'You have made everything quite clear now, have you not?' she asked gently, as she dispensed the wine to her visitors with her usual hospitable forethought and care.

'Perfectly so,' responded the elder of the two legal men; 'And if you will permit me to say so, I congratulate you, Lady Carlyon, on your strength of mind. Had the other will remained in force, your hardly-earned fortune would have soon been squandered.'

She answered nothing. After a little pause she spoke again.

'You quite understand that, in the event of my death, you yourself take possession of my last manuscript, and place it personally in the hands of my publishers?'

'Quite so. Everything shall be carried out in exact accordance with your instructions.

'You think,' she went on hesitatingly—'that I have given him enough to live upon?'

'More than enough—more than he deserves, said the lawyer. 'To be the possessor of two hundred and fifty a year for life is a great advantage in these days. Of course,' and he laughed a little, 'he'll not be able to afford tandem-driving and the rest of his various amusements, but he can live comfortably and respectably if he likes. That is quite sufficient for him.'

'He has already a sum in his own private bank, which, if placed at interest, will bring him in more than another hundred,' said Delicia, meditatively. 'Yes, I think it is sufficient. He cannot starve, and he is sure to marry again.'

'But you talk as if you were going to leave us at once and for ever, Lady Carlyon,' and the old lawyer looked somewhat concerned as he observed the extreme pallor of her face and the feverish splendour of her eyes. 'You will live for many and many a long day yet to enjoy the fruit of your own intellectual labours—'

'My dear sir, pray do not talk of my "intellectual labours!" In the opinion of my husband and of men generally, especially unsuccessful men, these very labours have rendered me "unsexed." I am not a woman at all, according to their idea! I have neither heart nor feeling. I am simply a money-making machine, grinding out gold for my "lord and master" to spend.'

Her lawyer looked distressed.

'If you remember, I told you some time back that I thought you were unaware of your husband's extravagance,' he said. 'I put it as "extravagance,"—because I was unwilling to convey to you all the rumours I had actually heard. Men are naturally fickle; and my experience is that they always take benefits badly, thinking all good fortune their right. You made a mistake, I consider, to trust Lord Carlyon so completely.'

'What would you have of me?' asked Delicia, simply. 'I loved him!'

There followed a silence. Nothing could be said to this, and the two men of the law munched their biscuits and drank their wine hastily, conscious of a sudden excitement stirring in them,—a strange impulse, moving them both to the desire of thrashing Lord Carlyon, which would be an action totally inconsistent with legal custom and procedure. But the sight of the fair, grave, patient woman who had worked so hard, who held such a high position of fame, and who was so grievously wronged in her private life, had a powerful effect upon even the practical and prosaic disposition of the two men born to considerations of red tape and wordy documents; and when they took their leave of her it was with a profound deference and sympathy which she did not fail to notice. Another time their evident interest and kindliness would have moved her, but now she was so strung up with feverish excitement and eagerness to finish the work she had begun, that external things made very little impression upon her.

She returned to her writing with renewed zest; Spartan was her chief companion; and only her maid Emily began to notice how ill she was looking. She had intended to consult a doctor about her health; but, absorbed in her work, she put it off from day to day, promising herself that she would do so when her book was finished. She received no news whatever from her husband; he was trying the effect of a lengthy absence and sustained silence on her always sensitive mind.

And so the days went on, through all bright June and the warm beginning of July, till one morning she entered her room prepared to write the last portion of what she instinctively felt and knew would lift her higher among the cold pinnacles of fame than she had ever been. She was aware of a soft lassitude upon her,—a sense of languor that was more delightful than unpleasing; the beautiful repose that distinguishes a studious and deeply-thinking mind, which had been hers in a very great degree before her marriage, when, as single-hearted Delicia Vaughan, she had astonished the world by her genius, came back to her now, and the clouds of trouble and perplexity seemed suddenly to clear and leave her life as blank and calm and pure as though the shadow of a false love had never darkened it. The sun fell warmly across her desk, flickering over the pens and paper; and Spartan stretched himself full length in his usual place in the window-nook with a deep sigh of absolute content. And with radiance in her eyes and a smile on her lips, Delicia sat down and wrote her 'conclusion.' Her brain had never been clearer,—thoughts came quickly, and with the thoughts were evoked new and felicitous modes of expression, which wrote themselves, as it were, without an effort on her own part.

Suddenly she started to her feet;—a great and solemn sound was in her ears, like the stormy murmur of a distant sea, or the beginning of a grand organ chant, gravely sustained. Listening, she looked wildly up at the dazzling sunlight streaming through her window pane. What strange, what distant Glory did she see, that all the light and all the splendour of the summer day should seem, for that one moment, to be mirrored in her eyes? Then—she gave a sharp, choking cry, . . .

'Spartan! Spartan!'

With one bound the great dog obeyed the call, and sprang up against her, putting his huge, soft paws upon her breast. Convulsively she clasped them close,—as she would have clasped the hands of an only friend,—and fell back heavily in her chair—dead!

So they found her an hour later,—her cold hands still holding Spartan's rough paws to her bosom,—while he, poor faithful beast, imprisoned in that death-grip, sat patiently watching his mistress with anxious and loving eyes, waiting till she should wake. For she looked as if she had merely fallen asleep for a few minutes; a smile was on her lips,— the colour had not quite left her face,—and her body was yet warm. For some time no one dared touch the dog, and only at last by dint of sheer force and close muzzling could they drag him away and lock him up in the yard, where he filled the surrounding neighbourhood with his desolate howling. He was 'only a dog;' he had not the beautiful reasoning ability of a man, who is able to console himself easily for the death of friends by making new ones. He had a true heart, poor Spartan! It is an unfashionable commodity, and useless, too, since it cannot be bought or sold. And when all the newspapers had headings—'Death of Delicia Vaughan,' with accounts of the 'sudden heart failure,' which had been the cause of her unexpected end, Lord Carlyon returned in haste to town to attend the funeral and to hear the will. But he found his presence scarcely needed,—for the great public, seized by a passionate grief for the loss of one of its favourite authors, took it upon itself to make the obsequies of this 'unsexed' woman as imposing as any that ever attended king or emperor. Thousands followed the coffin to the quiet Mortlake cemetery, where Delicia had long ago purchased her own grave; hundreds among these thousands wept, and reminded each other of the good actions, the many kindnesses that had made her suddenly-ended life a blessing and consolation to the sick and the afflicted, and many wondered where they should again find so true and sympathetic a friend. And when it came to be publicly known that all her fortune, together with all future royalties to be obtained from her books, was left in equal shares among the poverty-stricken of certain miserable London districts, with full and concise instructions as to how it was to be paid and when,—then callous hearts melted at the sound of her name, and eyes unaccustomed to weeping shed soft tears of gratitude and spoke of her with a wondering tenderness of worship and reverence as though she had been a saint. The Press made light of her work, and had scarce a word of sympathy for her untimely demise; their general 'tone' being that adopted by the late Edward Fitzgerald, who wrote of one of England's greatest poets thus:—'Mrs. Barrett Browning is dead. Thank God we shall have no more "Aurora Leighs!"' It is the usual manner assumed by men who have neither the brain nor the feeling to write an 'Aurora Leigh' themselves. All the same, the public 'rushed,' in its usual impulsive fashion, for the last book Delicia had written, and when they got it, such a chorus of enthusiasm arose as entirely overwhelmed the ordinary press cackle and brought down the applauding verdict of such reasoning readers and sober judges who did not waste their time in writing newspaper paragraphs. Delicia's name became greater in death than in life; and only one person spoke of her with flippant ease and light disparagement; this was her husband. His indignation at finding her fortune entirely disposed of among 'charities' was too deep and genuine to be concealed. He considered his allowance of two hundred and fifty a year an 'insult,' and he became an ardent supporter of the tyrannic theories of the would-be little Nero of Germany, who permits a law to be in active force which unjustly provides that all the earnings of wives shall belong to their husbands. He considered the painter-poet-composer-autocrat of the Fatherland an extremely sensible person, and wished such a law might be carried into effect in England. He forgot all Delicia's tenderness, all her beauty, all her intelligence, all her thoughtfulness and consideration for his personal comfort; and all her love counted as nothing when set against the manner in which he considered he had been 'done' in the results of his marriage with an 'unsexed' woman of genius. But gradually, very gradually, by some mysterious means, probably best known to Lady Brancewith, who had never forgiven the slight inflicted on her by his look and manner when he suddenly refused to drive home with her after promising to do so, rumour began to whisper the story of his selfishness, and to comment upon it.

'He had committed no crime. Oh, no,' said society, beginning to waver in its former adoration of his manly perfections, 'but he broke his wife's heart! Yes, that was it! How he did it nobody quite knew; there was something about the "Marina" woman at the "Empire," but nothing was quite certain. Anyhow, she died very suddenly, and Lord Carlyon was away at the time.'

And as people nowadays hardly ever express regret for a person's death, but immediately ask 'What money has been left behind?' the gossips had ample food for reflection, in the fact that nearly forty thousand pounds was Delicia's legacy to the poor.

'She must have had a very noble nature,' said the world at last, when the shrieking pipe of irritated criticism had died away, and when from the dark vista of death Delicia's star of fame shone clear, 'Her husband was not worthy of her!'

And Paul Valdis, stricken to the soul with a grief beyond expression, heard this great verdict of the world finally pronounced, with an anguish of mind, and a despair as tragic as that of Romeo when he found his lady in her death-like sleep.

'Too late, too late! My love, my darling!' he groaned in bitterness of spirit. 'What is it worth, all this shouting of praise over your silent grave? Oh, my Delicia! All you sought was love; so little to ask, my darling, so little in return for all the generous overflow of your gifted soul! If you could have loved me; but no! I would not have had you change your nature; you would not have been Delicia had you loved more than once!'

And his eyes rested tenderly on the wistful companion of his musing, Spartan, who had been left to his care in a very special manner, with a little note from Delicia herself, which was delivered to him by her lawyers and which ran thus:—

DEAR FRIEND,
    Take care of Spartan. He will be contented with you, for he loves you. Please console him and make him happy for my sake.
                                                            DELICIA

Valdis knew that little letter by heart; it was more priceless to him than any other worldly possession.

'Spartan,' he said now, calling the faithful animal to his side and taking his shaggy, massive head between his hands, 'Out of the whole world that calls our Delicia "famous," the world that has gained new beauty, hope and joy from the blossoming of her genius,—only you and I loved her!'

Spartan sighed. He had become a melancholy, meditative creature, and his great brown eyes were often suffused with tears. Had he been able to answer his new master then, he might have said,—

'Honesty is an ordinary quality in dogs, but it is exceptional in men. Dogs love and are faithful; men desire, and with possession are faithless! Yet men, so they say, are higher in the scale of creation than dogs. I do not understand this. If truth, fidelity and devotion are virtues, then dogs are superior to men; if selfishness, cunning and hypocrisy are virtues, then men are certainly superior to dogs! I cannot argue it out, being only a dog myself; but to me it seems a strange world!'

And truly it is a strange world to many of us, though perhaps the strangest and most incomprehensible part of the whole mystery is the perpetual sacrifice of the good to the bad, and the seeming continual triumph of conventional lies over central truths. But, after all, that triumph is only 'seeming'; and the martyrdom of life and love endured by thousands of patiently-working, self-denying women will bring its own reward in the Hereafter, as well as its own terrific vengeance on the heads of the callous egotists among men who have tortured tender souls on the rack, or burnt them in the fire, making 'living torches' of them, to throw light upon the wicked deeds done in the vast arena of Sensualism and Materialism. Not a tear, not a heart-throb of one pure woman wronged shall escape the eyes of Eternal Justice, or fail to bring punishment upon the wrong-doer! This we may believe,—this we MUST believe,—else God Himself would be a demon and the world His Hell!

THE END

A Note About the Author

Marie Corelli (1855–1924), born Mary Mackay, was a British writer from London, England. Educated at a Parisian convent, she later worked as a pianist before embarking on a literary career. Her first novel, *A Romance of Two Worlds* was published in 1886 and surpassed all expectations. Corelli quickly became one of the most popular fiction writers of her time. Her books featured contrasting themes rooted in religion, science and the supernatural. Some of Corelli's other notable works include *Barabbas: A Dream of the World's Tragedy* (1893) and *The Sorrows of Satan* (1895).

A Note from the Publisher

Spanning many genres, from non-fiction essays to literature classics to children's books and lyric poetry, Mint Edition books showcase the master works of our time in a modern new package. The text is freshly typeset, is clean and easy to read, and features a new note about the author in each volume. Many books also include exclusive new introductory material. Every book boasts a striking new cover, which makes it as appropriate for collecting as it is for gift giving. Mint Edition books are only printed when a reader orders them, so natural resources are not wasted. We're proud that our books are never manufactured in excess and exist only in the exact quantity they need to be read and enjoyed.

bookfinity™

Discover more of your favorite classics with Bookfinity™.

- Track your reading with custom book lists.
- Get great book recommendations for your personalized Reader Type.
- Add reviews for your favorite books.
- AND MUCH MORE!

Visit **bookfinity.com** and take the fun Reader Type quiz to get started.

Enjoy our classic and modern companion pairings!

Classic & Modern

Printed in the USA
CPSIA information can be obtained
at www.ICGtesting.com
JSHW082356140824
68134JS00020B/2099